# SACRED INK

## Get the Water Street Crime Starter Library
## FOR FREE

Sign up for the no-spam newsletter and get *four* full-length ebooks – the thrillers **BLOODY PARADISE, FROM ICE TO ASHES, TROPICAL ICE,** and **SING FOR THE DEAD** – plus two introductory short stories by the author of **STAINED FORTUNE** and lots more exclusive content, all for *free*.

## Details can be found at
## the end of SACRED INK,
## or go here now:

## https://mailchi.mp/waterstreetpressbooks.com/
## waterstreetcrimemailinglist

# SACRED INK

## A STORY OF PIETY... AND MURDER

# DAVID SNYDER

Published by Water Street Press
Healdsburg, California

Designer Credits
Cover art by **thecovercollection.com**

Interior design by **Anna Zubrytska**

Produced in the USA
Print 978-1-62134-428-5
E-Pub 978-1-62134-429-2
Mobi 978-1-62134-430-8

*Sacred Ink is dedicated to Beverly and Sarah*

# Acknowledgements

**A** published first novel is like a turtle on a fencepost. The animal had a lot of help getting there. The same is true for _Sacred Ink_. Deciding to write fiction later in life required a lot of patience, both on my part and on the part of the teachers and workshop participants who, over the years, have taught me the craft of writing and good storytelling. Thank you to all the many teachers who have critically read my work, including but not limited to Sharon Oard Warner, Tom Jenks, Carol Edgarian, Patricia Henley, Abby Frucht and the faculty of Vermont College of Fine Arts. Thank you to all the many readers and students who have read and commented on my work especially Pricilla Hoback and Margaret Wrinkle who heard _Sacred Ink_ from its inception, also Roger Skipper, Seth Biderman, Gregg Owens. I also thank Doug Casebeer, Randy Johnston, Jan McKeache, Sam Harvey and the remainder of the ceramic artist community who have been so encouraging over the years. Thank you to Lynn Vannucci for helping shape the story into its present form. Most of all thank you to my wife Vicki for being my best cheerleader and best critic.

# Good Friday,

*Tres Mujeres, New Mexico, 1995*

## Adolfo

This he remembered – that he'd shivered with thirty men in the predawn cold outside the *morada*, their long shadows twisted beneath an Easter moon. Some were old and wore white tunics and red bandanas tied around their necks; others were young and wore white cotton pants held at the waist with a rope, their upper bodies bare. All of them were tough and muscular and lived hard lives. They carried whips made of woven yucca. He wasn't part of the procession, only a spectator, a first-timer, but even his nerves jumped with anticipation.

He had come to these mountains with his art school roommate, Alex, who had grown up in Tres Mujeres. Throughout the drive from Los Angeles, Alex had talked on and on about the other part of this mountain village – *chiva*, and the crazy life. But Alex's father was mayor of the local chapter of *los penitentes,* and had invited them to attend.

"We don't have to be here, Adolfo," Alex said. He had seen his father perform this Easter ritual all his life; the mystery had been revealed to him and he'd found it wanting. Adolfo had only heard stories about the *penitentes*; he had to bear witness.

"You go then," Adolfo told him. Alex's father turned from his place at the head of the gathering procession and sighed when he heard Adolfo speak.

"Suit yourself." Alex sprinted off to his pickup.

The men assembled three abreast. In the front row, Alex's father was flanked to the right by a man Adolfo would learn was the *rezador*, who read the prayers, and on the left by a flute player. At the very front, walking alone, was a man not much older than Adolfo. His tangled hair was pulled back from his forehead, and goose bumps pimpled his brown, bare skin. The muscles in his arms and back were already tight from holding upright the eight-foot cross made of hand-hewn *vigas* that rested over his shoulder. Jesus. His left hand cradled the joint of the cross, the muscle of his forearm twitching under an elaborate tattoo of the Virgin of Guadalupe. The sky above Tres Mujeres peaks brightened, but even in the predawn light, Adolfo saw the colors of the tattoo were exquisite.

Three rifle shots broke the silence and the procession began slowly up the rocky, mile-long trail, winding its way through a canopy of pine trees. The *rezador* recited the prayers in a four-count rhythm. On the downbeat of each stanza, the bare-chested men slapped their backs with their woven whips. *Whack*, two, three, four. *Whack*, two, three, four.

Adolfo found himself walking with the rhythm. He was a wiry kid, and had routinely hiked the Sierras, but this morning his pulse was rapid, his lungs heavy. Between stanzas someone toward the front shouted, "For the sins of our village." Blood dripped down the back of the man in front of him. Adolfo had begun to sweat. He removed his fleece and shirt and tied them around his waist.

The man beside him handed him a fresh whip. "I make them," he whispered. "This one is extra."

Adolfo accepted the gift.

The four-foot whip was lighter than he'd expected. A splinter of the woven handle pierced his thumb. On his first whack a thousand needles raked his skin and tears filled his eyes, but on the next downbeat he struck himself again. Like the others he leaned into the hill, and with only another beat he was in unison with the other *penitentes*. The path steepened, and loosened rocks tumbled down behind him.

Jesus stumbled and Alex's father rushed to his aid. In his mind, Adolfo saw Caravaggio's *Flagellation of Christ*, not as spectator in a museum, but as participant, a world away from the one in which his sister had brought him up – the Easter seasons he'd known with her, the piety of Easter bonnets and padded kneelers. Two rows ahead of him one of the marchers moaned. Someone else called out, "Free us from addiction!" *Chiva*, Adolfo thought. The other part of this mountain village.

*Whack*, two, three, four. *Whack*, two, three, four. Labored breath rose like fog over a mountain pond.

The morning sun was now above Tres Mujeres peaks. The dissonant flute melody seemed to bounce off the bands of sunlight streaming through the trees. Adolfo's heaviness had lessened. His whip was weighted with sweat and blood. Adolfo realized he was the only one wearing shoes.

Beyond the steepest part of the trail the trees opened for Adolfo to see twenty women processing the perimeter of a white frame church. They were led by a small woman dressed all in white and holding aloft a heavy three-foot plaster statue of the Blessed Virgin. On either side of her two adolescent girls, also dressed in white, carried cloths the size of large handkerchiefs that had been imprinted with Christ's face. The women behind this trio wore hooded shawls of rough cotton. By the time Jesus had cleared the trees, the women had processed through the back door of the church, and inside.

The men entered through the front door, separating into the pews, leaving Jesus alone in the center aisle, his cross still heavy on his shoulder. His hair was tangled now with sweat. Blood oozed from the purple bruise that had formed above his shoulder blade. He tried to kneel, reaching out and bracing his hand against the pew to steady himself. The small woman in white came to the altar rail and knelt before him. Mary. The fourth Station of the Cross. This Mary had high cheek bones, and large black eyes. Her face was taut and sorrowful, and when she placed her hands on her son's face, her earthly pleading was nothing like the angelic depictions Adolfo remembered from his youth.

The men's faces were slick, their breathing still heavy. The odor of bodies mingled with the metallic scent of blood in the small church. A fresh breeze pushed through the front door as the congregants knelt for final prayers.

When they rose again. Adolfo joined the singing.

> *In your spirit thought so patient*
> *Pierced with anguish unrelenting*
> *Ran the sword of suffering love.*

The sanctuary was silent. Cheeks were streaked with tears.

After the ceremony, wooden folding tables were set up in the front lawn, draped with paper tablecloths and laden with coffee, tortillas, and burritos, and the solemnity quickly vanished. The conversations were lively – spring planting to *acequia* cleanup to who was coming home for the holiday. Adolfo was promptly captured by Alex's father.

"Welcome," he said. "Join us now as we break our fast, and join us later this morning for the stations of the cross. The pilgrims walking from Santa Fe will be here soon and we'll walk with them up the mountain, to the crosses. And"—he handed Adolfo a small tin of ointment—"use this on your back. It'll keep down the scarring."

"Thank you," Adolfo said, taking his eyes from the man seated across from him at the table for only a moment. Since leaving the church, Jesus had donned a tunic, but his forearms were bare, the tattoo still visible. Adolfo had only seen rude black or dark-green tattoos, pricked into willing skin by fellow art students in the dorms. The fine detail and the jewel colors on Jesus's arm enthralled him. Now in his third year of study, Adolfo had yet to dedicate himself to a medium. He was committed to figurative art, but flat surfaces left him cold. The tattoo made him wonder if living skin was his ultimate canvas. Before he could walk over to ask Jesus for a closer look, however, the whip-maker was at his side.

"My name is Efrin," he said.

"Oh…" Adolfo realized the whip was still in his hand.

"No, no," Efrin said. "Your blood has stained it and made it yours."

Before Adolfo could realize the enormity of his pleasure in this pronouncement, Alex stumbled toward them, eyelids half closed over pinpoint pupils. Dream walking. A spot of blood marked the injection site on his forearm. Alex's father was beside his son in a moment, lifting him by his collar, shoving him so he slid, on hands and knees, across the gravel path.

"You embarrass me," Alex's father spat.

In slow motion, Alex righted himself, brushing dirt from his jeans and blood from his elbows. Pointing his finger at his father, he let out a single, hollow, "Ha!" Then bellowed, "You think you know shit."

Alex had taken a fighter's stance, too wobbly to pose a threat beyond continuing to soil the day. Adolfo had no choice but to help him down from the mountain and back to L.A.

That summer Adolfo withdrew from art school. He went first to East L.A. to study with several ink masters, then after Thanksgiving he took a job in Honolulu to learn color and shading. The following spring, flush with talent and new skills, and yearning to be taken in by the *penitentes*, he returned to Tres Mujeres.

This much, he remembered.

# Fifth Friday of Lent,

*April 2004*

## Jimmy

The El Paso office of the FBI was located on the fifth floor of the Federal Justice Center on South Mesa Hills Drive, just East of I-10. Jimmy Montaño's corner space was not much larger than a broom closet. An air conditioner occupied the only window. A single, dog-eared file was the only item on the top of the metal desk. A long-time undercover agent, Jimmy checked in only when changing assignments.

Jimmy had lunched with his boss – roasted corn from a street vender, and a kernel skin had wedged itself behind his upper incisor. He rummaged in the desk drawer in search of a toothpick.

"Lookin' for these?" Fred Mullins, Special Agent-in-Charge, blocked the doorway, a box of toothpicks in one hand, working one around his lower molars with the other. "Love that roasted corn. Like everything good, it does require effort."

Jimmy reached for the box, taking one for now, three more for the road. The relief was immediate.

"Lubbock dispatch doesn't know you're one of us." Short and heavy set, Mullins was suited for little more than giving instructions to agents he treated as if they were fresh from Quantico.

"Fred, I got it." Jimmy stuffed his gun and badge into the battered leather messenger-style briefcase that rested on the desk chair. "I'm ten years into this.

"Antonio Sanchez from Uvalde."

"Fred, I said, I've got it." Most cases, Jimmy loved the new identities, getting into character. This time of year, though, Holy Week, he craved the identity he'd carved out in Tres Mujeres, where so much was unfinished. He raised his right arm and pushed up the sleeve. The multicolored Lady of Guadalupe tattoo was elaborate even for El Paso. "Maybe I should wear a wife-beater. This beauty would get me closer to the dealers."

"But not the truckers."

Official policy forbid agents from getting tattoos. Out here it was a necessity. Jimmy loved the way his beauty connected him with the culture of his youth. The *penitentes*. And the *chiva*.

Fred's big belly brushed against Jimmy as he made his way into the small office to inspect the file on his desk. "Let it go," he said, tapping the file, switching the toothpick from one side of his mouth to the other.

"I can't. I played it too loose and three people are dead. Plus, the killers are still at it, hiding behind the badge."

"Every agent has one." Fred tossed his toothpick into the waste can beside the desk, the wood making a hollow *ping* as it hit the empty metal bucket. "Fuggetaboutit." Fred laughed.

"All that work – and the evidence just disappeared." The setup had been natural, him returning to his own village north of Santa Fe, rigging up the old Airstream as a flop house. Hell, he'd even been able to use his old nickname, got to be Tito for a while. But the set-up had ended in a triple murder. Three years ago, during Holy week.

Palm Sunday was in a few days. "You're sending me on this new gig so I won't head up there to stir things up."

"Those boys'll fuck up sooner or later." Fred tossed Jimmy a ring of keys. "It's the only Kenworth in the lot."

Jimmy caught the keys and picked his vented ball cap from the arm of the desk chair, along with his leather brief case. He had plenty of time to get to Midland by this evening, get his load and drop it in Levelland by tomorrow noon. He'd studied the map and had spotted a few out-of-the-way truck stops and diners where he'd begin his queries.

"Cut that fucking pony tail," Fred hollered.

Jimmy turned at the stairs and laughed. "It goes with my shiny boots and leather jacket. I'm hundred-percent trucker."

"Where's the big belly?" Fred hollered back.

Before disappearing down the hall, Jimmy flipped his boss the finger.

The Kenworth was a twenty-year-old silver rattletrap, nothing like the luxury beasts long haulers drove these days. Jimmy plugged his music player into the radio and selected the day's playlist, Ranchero Music – perfect for hunting down Chihuahaun drug dealers. He adjusted the seat and turned the ignition. The truck fired immediately. Clutch to the floor, he found first gear. When he eased off the clutch and pressed the gas it popped into neutral. Three more tries and he was out of the parking lot.

On I-10, he passed the turnaround for Santa Fe and places north. Tito's Airstream was still up there. He momentarily took his foot off the gas—two-hundred-seventy miles straight up the Rio Grande, he could make it by nightfall—but, like forgetfulness, disobedience wasn't his nature, so he settled in with a flotilla of tankers heading east, back to the oil fields.

## Beth

That same morning and miles to the east, in Austin, in a yellow clapboard house in the Allendale part of town, Beth Rainey sat at her kitchen table. If she had looked up and through the picture window, she would have seen clusters of bluebonnets bobbing in the vacant lot next door, but Beth was not often distracted by pleasures. She squinted hard through a pair of reading glasses at an insurance form whose type was so fine she had drawn the document nearly to her nose. In the periphery of her attention, she heard her daughter upstairs getting ready for school—humming to herself as was her habit, a dance step executed on the tile floor while she ran a brush through her curly black hair in front of the bathroom mirror, a quiet moment to inspect the skin that freckled in the sun for blemishes, an application of the retinoic acid Beth had asked Raylon to prescribe more for Maggie's peace of mind than any real problem with her complexion. Beth's eyes ached—the fine print, she told herself—and she closed them. She only heard Maggie stumble into the kitchen as her flip-flop caught on a curl of the linoleum. Maggie grasped a corner of the counter so she wouldn't fall.

"I'll have that fixed before the For Sale Sign goes up," Beth said, removing her glasses and massaging her brow.

When Maggie didn't reply, Beth waved the document she still held her hand. "Our new health insurance plan." Beth was Clinical Director of Austin's East Side AIDS Clinic. She'd accepted a similar position at the Gulf Coast Clinic in Rockport, a small bayside town filled with tourists in the summer, retirees in the winter. She planned to move as soon as Maggie had graduated high school. Six weeks. "It's essentially the same plan we have here, so… No worries on that score."

Maggie offered a shrug while she poured Coco Puffs into a cereal bowl and added milk.

Beth looked out the kitchen window, still not seeing the bluebonnets, choosing her battles, not mentioning the holes in the knees of her daughter's faded jeans, or the oversized University of Texas jersey that hid from the world the fact that Maggie was an eighteen-year-old woman.

"I was thinking, since next week is Easter break, you and I could take a road trip to Rockport. Check out their community college. It's only a two-hour drive—"

Maggie let her spoon splash into her breakfast bowl.

"Jeanine drove me to the cemetery, yesterday," she said without looking up. "I put fresh lilies on Daddy's grave." Her father had been Director of Liturgy and Worship for St. Pious Catholic Church. Yesterday was the second anniversary of his death.

Beth nodded. Six weeks until her duty was done—until Maggie was graduated from St. Pious High School, where she and her father had agreed she would go. Six weeks until she could take her daughter away, and the two of them could begin a life outside the circle of grief they lived in now. "I'm sure your... Daddy appreciates that."

"I miss him, but I didn't cry."

Beth allowed herself a smile. "Well, that's progress. It's a sign you're ready to move on, I think."

"Move on." Maggie stared into her bowl, the sugary balls of cereal leaching chocolate-colored dye into the milk. "That's what you're supposed to do, right, after someone dies?" she asked. Then added, "Most people wait until after the actual death to do it, though."

"Please don't come down on Raylon," Beth said, closing her eyes again. It always helped to close her eyes when she was asked to recall the image of her daughter's face on the day after her father's death, when she caught Raylon leaving Beth's bedroom in the early morning hours. "Not now."

Maggie shoved her cereal bowl to the center of the table, splashing brown milk on the wood. "It's cool. Really. It used to not be, but today it's fine. He can stay over, move in, whatever. Do what you want."

Beth reached blindly across the table, afraid to look at Maggie. "Your dad was sick for *six years*. Someone had to work to provide for us. I did what I had to do—"

"Really, Mom, I'm fine." Maggie maneuvered away as Beth's hand came within an inch of closing on her arm.

Beth nodded, looking out the window again, at the blur of life outside this house where her husband had died, the haze of the future. "Will you go to Rockport with me next weekend? We can look for our new house, and your new school, and maybe a job for you too—"

"I have job," Maggie said. "And I'm not going to a crummy community college just because that would be convenient for you, and I'm not moving to *Rockport*."

She picked up her cereal bowl and tossed it in the sink. "You go ahead and move to East Buttfuck, Texas, if that's where you want to live, but I'm eighteen. You can't make me do anything anymore."

Beth didn't protest. Maggie was right; there was little a mother would be able to do if her eighteen-year-old daughter refused her. Even the medical concerns—Maggie's premature birth, the month she'd spent on a ventilator, the lifetime of delicately balanced health that dictated, even at her age, that she spend another year or two in her mother's care—even these were no longer legally accountable.

Beth didn't protest. She let Maggie walk out the kitchen door. The move to Rockport was a battle she didn't have to choose—at least not on this fine early morning when bluebonnets bobbed in the spring breeze.

As Beth looked out through the window into the vacant lot next door, Maggie returned to the kitchen and asked, "You have choir practice tonight, right?"

"Of course. Easter's just a week away."

"Well, then, remember… the senior trip. I'll be gone for the weekend by the time you get home."

"Right," Beth said. Six weeks, she thought. Six weeks to make Maggie see reason.

## Maggie

Maggie dropped her backpack to the sidewalk and grabbed the pole of the bus sign, leaned outward as if it were a draw rope on a catapult. She and her mom had been through so much together, and she understood completely the need her mother felt to be away from Austin, the St. Pious community, all those people who thought of the two of them as cripples because her father had died. She also knew that another year or two of living with her mother, continuing to go to school at some community college, wasn't going to change anything of importance, no matter where they spent those years.

"I'll still be the stupid girl who solves calculus equations in her head but can't read," Maggie had said the last time they'd talked about Rockport.

"You can read," Beth had replied.

"You know what I mean!"

Maggie let go of the sign. The rusted metal squawked, the sound of high-flying geese in a northward V, as the bus pulled into the stop, belching toxic fumes and promising freedom. Inside the bus, for thirty minutes, five days a week, two times a day, to and from school, she blended with everyone else going off to school, to work, to the shopping mall, doing regular things. On the bus she was one of them, not special or challenged, not the gifted math whiz or the daughter of a dead church hero, and nobody was waiting for her to come apart from grief. No one on the bus knew that the high point of her life so far had been the six years she'd spent taking care of her dying father. No one on the bus knew her at all.

No one except her best friend Jeanine, who was sitting in her habitual tenth-row window seat. Today Jeanine was dressed in oversized painter's pants, cream-colored with a gold chain running from the wallet in the side pocket to the belt loop in front. Her neatly pressed black cotton shirt was buttoned at the collar. Maggie referred to Jeanine as a fashion plate for skaters. Despite the baggy look, Jeanine was a stickler for details. Today she'd painted a green streak down the center of her spiky blond hair.

Maggie flopped onto the seat beside her.

Jeanine leaned over, pitching her voice so it was low and ghoulish, and said, "Tell me your secrets. All of them."

"You know them all." The bus lurched away from the curb.

"Often before you do," Jeanine agreed, pointing to a set of invisible boxes. "Which one should I choose? One, two, or three? Today it's number three. A set of keys for a band-new red Mustang! Hey, tell you what, after school let's take yours for a drive. I'll help you with the left turns off Lamar onto 19th. Whatta ya say, Mags?"

She turned her back to Jeanine. She'd had the Mustang for six months, a birthday gift from her mother. Her first day out she'd stalled the engine trying to turn left off Burnett Road, backing up traffic for six blocks. People had honked their horns and screamed at her. "Stupid bitch, learn to fucking drive!" Her fear of left turns in heavy traffic kept the Mustang in the garage. "How did you know?" she asked.

Jeanine shrugged. "I've seen Adolfo's low-riding Dodge Charger. It just makes sense you'd take your brand-new car and not his piece of crap."

"Yeah," Maggie admitted. "Right."

"I mean, you want to get where you're going, don-cha? Of course you're taking your car—"

"OK, OK. Stop." She rifled through her backpack and handed Jeanine three neatly folded sheets of paper. "Here. Your algebra assignment. I messed-up problem three on purpose."

In return, Jeanine handed over a brown envelope containing an original essay on the odes of John Keats. "I finished it last week, so if you want to turn it in."

Maggie and Jeanine were mirrored pieces of the same puzzle—what one lacked, the other had in spades. Jeanine was all about the words, claiming that when she had meningitis at age three the number section of her brain had disappeared. Despite her difficulties with reading, Maggie was gifted in math, or, more than gifted—numbers came to her alive, adding, subtracting, multiplying, dividing on the own. Calculus solutions appeared fully formed.

"You do this better than Mr. Conrad." Jeanine slipped the algebra assignment into her own backpack.

"Just don't ask me to explain how I came up with the solutions." The bus turned left. Maggie held onto the seat in front of her to keep form sliding into Jeanine. "Jee? Am I horrible, leaving my mother without a word, letting her find out I've gone when I don't show up back home from the senior trip?" It wasn't that she didn't love her mother; you didn't stop loving someone because you were annoyed with her.

Because she'd been too busy worrying about her own career that she'd had no time to care for her dying husband.

Because she'd left the caretaking to a ten-year-old kid.

Because now that he was dead, she'd decided it was time for her to have a change of scenery, and she was bullying her daughter into going along with her plans as if Maggie were still ten years old and not allowed an opinion about what her own future might look like.

Maggie shook her head. She'd been annoyed with her mother for years on end. "Maybe I should write her a note. Leave it somewhere I'm sure she won't find it until Monday morning?"

"Give it to me," Jeanine offered. "I'll deliver it. I'll be in the middle of it all anyway."

Maggie narrowed her eyes. "You *want* to be in the middle of it."

Jeanine giggled. "OOH-LA-LA. That's my word of the day. What do you call him? Is he your boyfriend? Your lover? Your consort? Are you his concubine?"

"Don't talk like that," Maggie snapped. Besides not knowing what 'concubine' meant, she was unsure herself what exactly to call Adolfo. She certainly wasn't his lover. Not yet. They'd kissed, of course, and talked about doing more, but he was sick and his meds took away not only his desire to perform sexually, but his ability to do so. And his illness made her wary about appropriate precautions. Her mother worked in AIDS care, and she'd made sure that Maggie knew what to do, what not to do, how to do it, no sex with a drug user, always insist on a condom, oral sex leads to throat cancer… One more safe sex lecture and Maggie thought she'd go mad with the repetition of it all.

She didn't *care* that Adolfo had AIDS. She didn't want him to be sick, of course. But she couldn't deny that part of his appeal was that she would get to take care of him, the way she'd taken care of her dad.

The day she met him, at Whole Foods, she had been stocking fruit and accidentally spilled a box of kiwis. The little brown balls rolled all over the produce section. Out of nowhere, Adolfo appeared, laughing as he helped gather the fruit before the store manager—who the employees referred to as Mr. Capone—could find out what had happened. After their shift, Adolfo bought her a cappuccino at the store's coffee bar. She talked about music—that week it had been all John Coltrane and Snoop-Dog. She told him how she counted the notes, or, not really counted them, not what most people thought was counting. She told him how numbers flashed in her mind, multicolored, so many notes per phrase, the number of repetitions, another group for the verse—red, green, blue—and so on, numbers in combination of brilliant colors, adding, subtracting, until by the end of a song she'd have a full array of them, vibrating and pulsing.

"Synesthesia." Adolfo smiled.

"I don't like being a syndrome." She smiled back at him, as she hadn't when her mother and Raylon gave her the same diagnoses.

Adolfo had talked about his body art and a magical place called Tres Mujeres in the mountains of New Mexico.

"There's a place he knows," Maggie said.

"Yes?" Jeanine encouraged.

"A place where we can live, out in the woods—"

"A cabin!"

"With a fireplace!"

"And a braided rug in front of it..."

"It's just standing empty, Adolfo says, waiting for us!"

"OOH-LA-LA!"

Laughing, Maggie grabbed Jeanine's arm. "I'll write my mom a note, and you won't give it to her until you're back from the senior trip?"

"Consider me part of your conspiracy." Jeanine's eyes were brown like chocolate, and in them, Maggie saw she meant every word of her promise.

# Adolfo

He smelled burning piñon, heard ravens cawing in the windy pine boughs. He was an artist, a *hermanos,* a member of the local *morada.* He had friends. People came to him for the ink or *chiva* or just to crash. And a girl, Rachel, loved him.

Adolfo awakened, heart pounding as if he'd run a hundred-yard dash. It took him several moments, eyes wide and darting around the small efficiency apartment where he lived above his sister's garage, to get control of his nerves, and orient himself.

He was already packed, his duffle on the floor stuffed with flannel shirts and a puffy down parka for the mountain cold, black cowboy boots with silver caps on the pointed toes as befit a popular Southwestern artist. The metal tackle box beside it contained art supplies—brushes, paints, charcoal pencils, along with his tattoo gun, needles, and bottles of ink. His black portfolio, filled with drawings and paintings and tattoo designs, many of which dated from art school, leaned against the wall.

He didn't think about Maggie until he was shuffling barefoot to the bathroom. It bothered him that she liked him more than he liked her. It bothered him that he needed her. He was sick and she knew how to nurse sick people—she had as much as admitted she *liked* nursing her dying father. What kept him distant from her, he believed, was the problem of sex. Now that they'd be living together, she'd want it even more than she already did and he was useless as long as he was on these *pinche* medicines.

Amber pill bottles lined the glass shelf above the iron-stained bathroom sink. All of them, except for the hydrocodone, had been recently refilled. In the mirror, he caught his gauntness, his thinning black hair. Loose skin had gathered at the base of his neck and, when he smiled to inspect his teeth, white patches like bits of cottage cheese clung to his gums. Gone for the last two years, the white patches had reappeared a month ago. He coughed and the awful metal taste spread from the back of his throat.

"A shadow-man at twenty-nine," he said aloud.

He glanced from the line of pill bottles back to the bedroom and the still-open duffle. Until this moment he'd never considered *not* taking his meds. Suddenly his return to Tres Mujeres, where for six years his life had made sense, seemed enough for him. The mountains would cure the foul taste in his mouth, the fever, the limp dick. And if he died while there? Awakening to the rustle of the wind in the aspen trees, the soft patter of chipmunks skittering through the fallen leaves, and the smells—pine and juniper, alfalfa, rain and thunder across the valley, piñon smoke. If that was all there was, so be it. Live or die, if it happened in the mountains, he was ready.

On the far end of the shelf was the blue velvet box of healing dirt taken from the *Sanctuario* in Chimayó.

Adolfo dipped his finger into it then made an awkward sign of the cross over his heart, a quick prayer for a safe journey—not to Jesus, but to the dirt itself. The box of dirt he put into his duffle and zipped it closed.

## Olivia

She knocked softly on the door to her garage apartment and, when there was no response, she followed the knock with a sweetly crooned, "Dolfi?" When she was again met with silence, Olivia, Adolfo's sister, slid open the door and peered around it. She was a stout woman whose brown tunic-style dress hung below ample knees, a silver crucifix pin dangled from an incongruous Peter Pan collar. Speaking in a whisper, as if she were in church, she called, "May I come in?" and stood still by the door waiting for an answer.

When none came for the third time, Olivia was relieved. Adolfo had been impatient and abrupt all his life, but in the last few months he'd been especially unforgiving. Especially, it seemed to Olivia, with her. When they crossed paths while she was leaving for daily mass or her Monday prayer group, he'd taunt, "Oh, there goes my holy sister! Go be holy and say some prayers for all of us sinners!" When she lamented that he was losing his faith and encouraged him to join the St. Pious men's group, he'd sneered at her, "Sure, sure, I want to hang around with some white-collar Anglos so I can watch them glad-hand each other about their own good works—pussy men who'd shrivel up if they ever had to show their faith like the *hermanos*!" She'd sensed for months that her brother was growing sick again. Then, the week before, when she'd noticed the reappearance of the white patches on his gums, she'd brought her prie-dieu up to his apartment, struggling with it on the stairs, in the hopes he'd turn back to prayer to cure the virus. Instead he'd been violent, almost destroying it in his haste to get it out when he'd come home and found it near his bed.

Alone in his apartment now, she looked around at the sparse furnishings, her eyes alighting on what she suspected she would find there: his duffle bag and his art supplies, packed and ready for escape. "Oh, Dolfi! Not now, not at Easter," she wailed.

For two decades Olivia had been the school nurse at St. Pious High School. Adolfo was the youngest of their parents' children, ten years younger than Olivia. She'd cared for him since he was a toddler, even taking him with her as if she was a young, single mother, when she set off for nursing school, helping him with his homework and cooking his meals and tucking him in at night in between her own studies. In the end, Olivia would understand his leaving. She always had. When he'd gone to art school, she'd collected money from their two sisters and brother for his tuition; and when he'd left school early to study body art, she'd repaid them, claiming the money had come from Adolfo himself. She was sorrowful now only because he hadn't trusted her enough to tell her himself that he was leaving. That he hadn't thought to spend the holiest of holidays with her, to wait until the school year was out in six weeks so Olivia could take him back to Tres Mujeres herself.

"I would do that for you, Dolfi," she vowed to the empty apartment, as she wiped her tears and unzipped her brother's duffle bag enough to stuff a handful of crumpled twenties inside.

## Beth

She had been raised on a West Texas cotton farm and thought of her life as marked by long horizons, traveling long roads that didn't bend. Early on, she became obsessed with getaways—not the leaving but the going, to anywhere that was different from where she was.

Soon after she'd married, she found a little suitcase that had an image of a DC-9 with a background of fluffy clouds embroidered on the side, at a backyard rummage sale. She'd kept it packed with two outfits, a night gown, and toiletries for a quick getaway—an impromptu overnight adventure with her new husband, a surprise weekend with her small family after Maggie was born, a promise to herself that she would be ever ready when life offered opportunity.

Such opportunities ended when her husband, Bill, was diagnosed with lymphoma. Maggie was ten at the time. Beth packed the little bag away. But two weeks ago, just after she'd received the offer for the new job in Rockport, she pulled down the attic door to search again for her little suitcase. Since it was loosely wrapped in newspaper, it had retained its luster. The silver threads of the propellers sparkled beneath the gold lamé sunshine. Beth packed the bag as she'd done years before and set it beside the dresser. This coming week, she'd take it on its first road trip in nearly a decade, with Maggie—and, perhaps, Raylon—to Rockport.

She could have daydreamed about her road trip far longer than she allowed herself. She was, at heart, a practical woman, and she was running late. Her meeting of the AIDS Coalition Board was in less than an hour. Today she planned to forego her usual report and give notice of her upcoming move. Her position would be hard for the board to replace—if pressed, she would agree to stay on until July first. For the occasion, she'd chosen her blue linen dress, a lucky, celebratory dress she'd purchased for her job interview in Rockport.

She reached behind to zip the dress as she on her way out of her bedroom and noticed the blue light on her answering machine was blinking.

"Bethie! It's Father Tom. We're on our way over to load up Bill's piano."

"Damn." More than Tom's timing, it was the way he always said her dead husband's name, "Bill," as if he'd been a modern-day holy man. Since his death, people at the church had looked upon her and Maggie as their special project, as if neither of them was quite capable of making it in a complicated world without Bill's holy intervention. For a time, she'd stopped attending Mass, hoping to avoid these people, but she needed the sacraments. And when the parish hired a new music director to replace Bill, a man who, unlike her dead husband, loved Bach and Mozart, she had rejoined the choir. What really annoyed her, even she admitted it only to herself, was the way Tom had appropriated Bill for his own. Tom had been *her* friend long before either of them had known a person named Bill Rainey existed in the world, but ever since Bill's death, it seemed as if their entire relationship had always been filtered through this third person.

Beth hurried down the stairs hoping to get away before Tom arrived, but he was already at the front door.

"How's my girlfriend?" He kissed her on the cheek. Like Beth, Tom had grown up in the Texas panhandle, and he'd been Beth's classmate at Boston College, where he'd lettered three years in basketball. Had they dated back then? Beth might have said at the time that was what they were doing, but she wasn't surprised when he left for the seminary.

"I'm late for a board meeting," she informed him now, standing in front of him on the small front porch and closing her door behind her.

"Ah—" He seemed taken back by her abruptness. "Sorry I couldn't let you know sooner, but I've just this morning had an offer of a truck and dolly."

"It's only three months since I donated the piano to the church."

"I can come back later—"

Beth waved his answer away. "Take the piano—just don't bring that hand-waving, praise music back into the church."

"We've got new people on the Parish Council, Beth. Not everyone remembers the glory of Bill's music."

"Does that mean I'm no longer an agenda item, that the holy groups will stop sending me prayer cards?"

"You've been my special project since college." Tom handed her the day's mail. "Your box was full. Never know when it's going to rain."

Beth sighed and reluctantly opened her front door so both she and Tom could enter. She thumbed through the various bills and catalogues before dropping the lot, save one, onto a table in the entry.

Tom noted the large, legal-sized manila envelope bearing the logo of the Gulf Coast Care Coalition still in her hand. "Your new job?"

"The final contract," she said, and then gave in and gave her old friend a smile. "Just holding it in my hand makes me feel as if I can smell a warm Gulf wind.

Tom nodded. "I still can't see you moving away, you know. This house belonging to someone else…" He smiled wickedly and added, "I heard the Rockport priest is a real dolt."

Beth grinned back at him. "I went online and found a wood-frame cottage on stilts with a deck reaching out over the bay—what a view! I can sit on my deck and paint marsh birds."

"I love your water colors," he said. "I still have the one you gave me in college—sunrise over a wooden oil derrick."

"And a far horizon," she added.

Tom shielded his eyes with his palm and stared into the distance. Having grown up in the high plains, he too understood the lure of them.

"I've got to go. Lock up when you're done."

"We all love you," Tom called after her, and watched her give her shoulders a shrug as she slid into her car.

The eight-year-old Subaru sputtered as she pulled away from the curb, died, then reluctantly restarted. Lately, the car had been doing that. Beth blamed it on the cheap gas she'd found out by the Montopolis Bridge. Beth's horizon remained a white frame house with a deck that reached over the bay, and she thought she'd better have the car serviced before she tried to drive it there.

## Adolfo

Adolfo arrived at the clinic with time to spare but was told to wait. Some meeting, the receptionist said. He started to tell her that his time was just as important as any doctor's, but he didn't want to piss her off. All he needed was a refill on his hydrocodone and, if that didn't work, then the cough syrup, Tussionex, the codeine-based jelly known on the street as "mellow yellow." Having a stash of either was money in the bank for the trip ahead; he could be as patient as he had to be, he supposed.

When they called his name, he grabbed his backpack and went first to the lab for his routine blood work, which included his current viral load, then to exam room three.

"Mr. Taranto," Beth greeted him. Her white coat was buttoned below the waist, a pink stethoscope hung around her neck.

"Nice dress, Mrs. Rainey." Maggie had told him of her mother's new job, of course, and the splurge for a new dress. "That blue's your color."

To him, his compliment sounded contrived, but Beth didn't seem to think so. She thanked him with a wide, bright smile, then opened his chart to the vital signs graph and told him to bare his arm. Adolfo pulled his sweater and Oxford cloth shirt, both of which he'd picked out of a Goodwill box, over his head in one piece. He didn't mind that his black cotton undershirt had holes in the armpits. After all, he was a starving artist. Without the added layers of clothing, he shivered.

Beth took his vitals. "You're down seven pounds in a month. Are you taking your pills?"

"Every day," he said, then coughed—a sound which, to his ears, seemed less contrived than the compliment.

"Keeps me up at night. And my ribs hurt so bad." He rubbed his chest as if that would prove his claim.

"At one-twenty-five, you can't lose any more." Beth touched his arm as if she knew what he'd done.

He hated the inference, no matter that it was correct. What did she know his life and struggles? He'd had friends with undetectable viral loads. Then, boom, everything would change overnight. The medicines, the cocktail plus the antibiotics with their sulfur taste, a med schedule that required two sets of alarm watches, the nausea, the midnight belches that tasted like rotten eggs, the daily runs that smelled like a dead person. He wanted to feel alive and, if he couldn't do that, he wanted it all to end. He felt good about what he'd done—like so many others, he'd thrown away his pills.

Adolfo forced a cough, a big wet one, then another, and another until he had given himself spasms. Beth poured him a glass of water. He complained that his chest pain was dragging him down, so Beth raised his T-shirt and listened, her stethoscope cold against his skin. As ever, she failed to comment on the multicolored tattoo of the Virgin Guadalupe that covered his back, from the base of his neck to his waist, which still surprised him. He didn't mind her disinterest—the Virgin was as much a part of him as his nose or hand—it was just that no one else who'd ever seen the art on his body had failed to gasp at its beauty.

He could tell from the face she made while she listened to his heart that she was concerned—hopefully enough to give him what he wanted. He forced another series of wet ones. A ball of sour phlegm lodged in his throat. He forced it down with the remainder of the water.

She handed him his shirt and sweater. "And what about refills?"

Adolfo moved his fist to his mouth and pretended to suppress another spasm. "Just got 'em, all except the hydrocodone and that cough syrup, you know, the jelly." He coughed again. She asked him to point to the pain. "In my ribs. It makes it hard to sleep."

Beth was accustomed to narcotic requests. Adolfo knew about the warning in his chart, No Narcotic Refills Except by Doctor. He coughed again, this time wincing to his side, holding his ribs. He wanted this to appear to be more than drug-seeking.

"I'll give you an appointment to see Dr. Caffey on Friday."

"Mrs. Rainey, that's the problem. By Friday I'll be gone," he said. "I'm blowin' this place and going back to my mountains."

"That's what you all say." Beth wrote out the appointment card. "Talk to Dr. Caffey about the cough. He may want a chest X-ray."

"Mrs. Rainey, I'm not kidding. By Friday I'll be gone. Can't you get me something now?" When he looked up at her with imploring brown eyes, she was smiling; Adolfo knew he'd won a small battle.

Beth reached into the cabinet drawer and handed over samples of the non-narcotic pearls. "Use these until you see the doctor."

"I'm serious about leaving, and these things never work," he said, shoving them back at her.

"Maybe you're right. They never did anything for my husband." Beth returned them to the cabinet.

For good measure, Adolfo delivered a deep, wet spasm.

"I'll have Dr. Caffey OK it and call in the Tussionex."

"What about my pain pills?"

"Don't count on it. If you're not coughing, the pain will go away." Adolfo let it go. If he pushed too hard, he'd lose the cough jelly as well. He hopped off the table then reached into his pack. From it, he withdrew a brown, paper-wrapped rectangle. "For you, always being nice to me and all."

Inside the wrapping, Beth found a water color of tall blue mountains covered with snow. "I know you paint, too. You said one time when I told you I was a tattoo artist. Those are my mountains where I'm going."

"This is beautiful, Adolfo. And so nice of you." Beth touched his arm. "Is there a clinic where you're going?"

"Yes. Remember, it's where I got my diagnosis. It's in my chart." Adolfo had told her so many things about his former life, including the name of the village where he'd lived, but she was always so focused on labs and vitals and symptoms, non-medical details never stuck. Part of him genuinely liked Maggie's mother, her manner of efficient compassion. Another part of him was less generous; this part of him thought, in a few days, she'll be wishing she'd paid better attention to me when I said things during our appointments.

## Beth

Beth bummed a Camel from the janitor and lit up on the back steps. A breeze pushed the thin line of smoke across the alley toward the vacant lot, a blend of bluebonnets and Indian paintbrush. She smoked only once or twice a week, but when Bill was alive, he would smell the contraband on her immediately and condescend, "What if the people of the parish knew?" The thought now made her laugh; she was certain he'd confided to his church groupies about her unholy habit.

A cigarette made her feel unencumbered, free of responsibilities, and she needed that right this moment. A gray ring drifted out her mouth and over the sidewalk. She turned her head as the clinic door opened.

"It's always the same," Raylon said as he joined her on the step.

"I don't know why you and Tolbert go through the exercise at this point."

Raylon raised his eyebrows, turning his blue eyes on her in such wide innocence that she laughed. "Oh, you know. He growls that we have to cut services if we're going to meet budget, and you growl back that we can't cut services just when our patient load is increasing; and then the two of you go at it in the board room like a couple of terrible lions and, in the end, one of you ponies up so we can keep the clinic doors open… Anyway," Beth flicked ashes onto the ground, "isn't it always the same?"

Raylon lifted the cigarette from her fingers and took a long draw. "Kids are coming in here younger and younger. They all think AIDS is ancient, like the plague, or tuberculosis. Take a few pills and it'll be fine. Nobody's using protection and, thanks to the churches, the city's shut down all the needle exchanges—"

"My contract came. Five days a week, a doctor from Corpus Christi on three of those. The good news is the clinic has one major benefactor, son died of it in the eighties, and he doesn't mind putting his hand in his pocket when the place comes up short at the end of the month."

Raylon took another drag of Beth's cigarette before handing it back to her. "Maybe I should follow you. Set up shop down the road in Corpus Christi." The smoke curled over his brow.

Beth and Raylon had been together, on and off, since before Bill's death. She liked that he enjoyed an occasional cigarette with her. And the curl his salt-and-pepper hair made over the collar of his blue Oxford cloth button-down. And the way his lanky frame fit around her when he spooned her after they'd made love. But the thought of their coming out as a couple in their tightly knit, gossipy, predominately Catholic area of town where her dead husband was still idolized in their parish, had always seemed too complicated to her. "I like that you're thinking of following me," she said. She expected the smile the idea inspired from her to be returned. When it was not, she said, "You lost somebody."

"Bennie," he reported.

"Little Bennie? The kid from South Austin who worked in his mother's gift shop?"

"Little, but not that young. He was thirty-four. Still, too young."

Beth nodded. "Not your fault."

"Keep telling me that."

Beth picked tobacco off her tongue. "Bennie missed his last two appointments."

"He stopped his meds a month ago. His mother took him to the hospital when he couldn't breath."

"Why do they do that?"

Raylon shrugged. "They get tired of the schedule, so many pills, and the way the pills make them feel. So they stop taking them—and for a week or two, they seem better. They feel better." Raylon's head fell forward, as if it were too heavy to hold. "Three or four at the most."

"Adolfo's given up, too," she said.

"What makes you say so?"

Beth inhaled deeply, and slowly expelled three luxurious rings before she replied. "He's kinder, more engaging," she said. "Plus he's running away to some-place in New Mexico where he lived before he got sick. He'll probably start doing heroin again. I'm pretty sure he's stopped his meds already." She threaded her arm through Raylon's and pulled him close. "I'd love you to follow me. Maggie and I are driving down to look at the community college next weekend. Maybe find her a job. Maybe you'll come with us?"

Raylon grinned. "And what do you think Maggie will say about that, if I do?"

"She'll come around," Beth told him, refusing to consider that her words might be only wishful thinking. "The three of us can do a crab boil on the beach and drink warm beer."

"That sounds like a dream."

Beth considered. She and her husband had never had a dream life—not any life she'd dreamed of—and, in the last year of it, he'd abandoned any attempt to fit her into what was left to him, preferring the company of his church groupies to hers. The simple, solid homeliness of starting a life with a man who enjoyed her company was thrilling.

"I've got choir practice tonight. You could come afterwards, stay the night."

"You think it's safe? I mean some of the church peo-ple might be watching from the bushes…"

"I don't give a shit if they set out surveillance cameras."

"What about Maggie?"

Beth smiled. "Maggie is off on her senior class trip to South Padre Island. We'll have the whole house to ourselves."

He slid his fingers into her thick black curls and pulled her head gently to him, kissing her on the cheek. "Tonight," he whispered.

Then the door cracked open, and she was alone on the stoop.

# Maggie

Ruiz's place was a shotgun store in a strip mall on Koenig, not far from Maggie's house. It had blackened windows with tidy white lettering, *Blue Tattoo*. A small bell on the door announced their entrance. The navy blue and white checkered tiles on the floor were so shiny they looked almost new, and the air smelled of alcohol and Pine-Sol. Maggie was surprised by the cleanliness.

At the counter was a short man wearing a black wife-beater over a weight-lifter's build. One of his arms was covered with small tattoos, in a pattern that looked to Maggie like a series of post-it notes, and around the other wrapped a thick rattlesnake done in almost iridescent greens, its fangs inked on the man's hard bicep, bared and ready to strike. Beside him was a tall woman who seemed, even standing still, to have a dancer's grace.

Her hair was cut in a shag and she was wearing a khaki shirt with "A-1 Trucking" embroidered onto the breast pocket. It seemed to Maggie as if she and Adolfo had interrupted something intimate between them, and also that they had been expected. The woman looked at Adolfo, then at Maggie, and then lifted her right leg to rest the toe on the counter that separated them. "At least tell me where you're going in case I need a touch up."

It appeared to Maggie, at first, that the woman was wearing multicolored tights patterned with a thorny rose bush, but what she was looking at was a tattoo, Adolfo's work, beginning at the woman's ankle and disappearing beneath her denim miniskirt.

"I'm Pearl," the woman said in a voice that made Maggie smell whiskey and weed. "This is Ruiz"—she jerked a thumb at the man in the wife-beater—"and you must be Maggie. This"—she pointed her toe and waved her knee—"is your boyfriend's latest masterpiece."

"Pearl…"

"Oh, don't pretend to be humble, honey." She laughed when Adolfo demurred. "My leg is the talk of the road from Albuquerque to Spokane." She floated her foot back to the floor. "So, you're a virgin to the ink?" Pearl asked. "Bet you've thought about it, though. Got a design picked out?"

Pearl was the kind of woman Maggie had only before seen at a distance, along Sixth Street. She was sorry she'd agreed to meet Adolfo here after her school day was over, and she was sorry her schoolgirl backpack, heavy with the books and tablets she'd had to take with her in order to avoid suspicion that she wouldn't be returning to school the following Monday, was slung over her shoulder. She folded her arms protectively and stepped back as she nodded. Her choice for her first tattoo, until that moment, had been a small Jack of Hearts on the inside of her left wrist, but she was suddenly embarrassed of it. Of how cliché it probably was. Of knowing that Pearl had once made a pass at Adolfo, but that he'd turned her down because of the problem his medication caused with his performance. Of the way Ruiz's eyes were rolling over her—the curve of her shoulder, the angle of her thigh, lingering at the valley between her breasts. He burst out laughing at the blood rushing to her cheeks and shoved a small, white envelope across the counter at Adolfo. "Pearl's last installment. You get the whole thing." Ruiz raised his hand for a high five. "My best assistant ever. Hell, man, if you weren't sick you mighta put me out of business."

Adolfo raised his right hand to accept the high five, but his left was clenched. Maggie grabbed onto his wrist with both hands. He'd made a joke about how the side effects of the meds had made it impossible for him to respond when Pearl had made her pass, but that his disease had relegated him to drawing designs on paper for someone else to execute on a customer's skin really pissed him off.

Adolfo shoved Maggie's grip away and stuffed the envelope into his back pocket. "I want my design portfolio too, Ruiz. Turn 'em over, bro. All of them."

Ruiz outweighed Adolfo by thirty pounds, and the snake flexed on his bicep, but he took measure of Adolfo's tone and reached under the counter. "Don't want you coming back and setting up shop down the street," Ruiz said, sliding two large folios across the counter to Adolfo. "Oh yeah, that's not possible because of the…"—Ruiz drew circles in the air with his index finger—"health certificate."

Adolfo drew back, his fingers twitching as if they wanted to make a fist. Maggie grabbed his arm again with one hand, and the folios off the counter with the other, and they fled.

Outside Adolfo spat. "He puts shit on skin! He has no art, no inspiration. No skill! And then he treats me like his boy?"

Maggie spun him around. "Not anymore," she said. "Not when we get to Tres Mujeres. Up there you can do your art for real."

## Beth

She was late. St. Pious was twelve blocks from Beth's home, north on Burnet Road then west on a series of narrow, winding streets. As she pulled into the parking lot, her car sputtered, then belched a black cloud out the tail pipe as she shifted gears into a stall.

The activities building was behind the high-shouldered church built of Texas limestone, and the rehearsal room was at the far end of the long first floor hallway lined with doorways to the classrooms used on Sundays for Baptismal and Confirmation classes. Her quick footsteps echoed off the tile floors as she jogged to the rehearsal room. She smiled to a litany of hellos and glad-you-could-make-its, took her music from the rack and joined Cecelia in the front row of the alto section on the bottom right of the three-tiered risers.

Beth was ready to lose herself in the Pascal music. Bill had believed that music in the church should be for the congregation to sing, so he ignored all the greats, and insisted on simple praise songs sung to guitar accompaniment. She tried not to dwell on his displeasure at the selections of the new choir director, but oh, she loved to sing Bach and Mozart. The choir was preparing St. Mathew's Passion, one of her favorites.

"Don't you love these selections?" she asked Cecelia, holding up the sheet music from the top of her stack. "'Ave Maria,'" she said, and not the sweet version sung at weddings. The arrangement she held was mournful and dissonant, a song of a mother and her loss, the cover page decorated with an embossed image of the Blessed Virgin's lovely, sorrowful face.

"I do," Cecelia Walton, Maggie's high-school guidance counselor, agreed, her head bobbing up and down on her thin neck, angled forward, in that odd way that had led Maggie to dub her the stork woman. "Do you know your Maggie hasn't made an appointment to see me yet about her college applications?"

Beth nodded, trying to imagine how such a meeting would ever happen. Maggie had long ago made it plain that she thought Cecelia was biased in favor of what she called the jocks and the prom queens, a group for which neither she nor Jeanine had any affinity, and so she had no use for Cecelia.

"We've decided she's going to live at home and attend a community college for a couple of years. She was a premature baby, and she's a young eighteen… That's all, Cecilia."

Cecelia nodded, and leaned sideways so Beth could hear her whisper, "Good. I was concerned it was that older boy she's been seeing."

Beth turned completely sideways to face Cecelia head on. "What boy?"

"You know Olivia, the school nurse? It's her younger brother. The one with the tattoo."

Beth gasped like a truck tire ripped by a blade. "Adolfo?"

"You know him?"

Forgetting her obligation for confidentiality, Beth bawled, "He comes to the clinic!"

Cecelia covered her mouth, but still her moan was loud enough to catch the attention of the choral director. "Ladies!" he barked, turning his attention from the soprano he was instructing on her solo.

# Adolfo

"Why is there a piano in your front yard?" Adolfo laughed.

Maggie rolled her eyes. "Who knows?" She laughed back. "Here." She'd unlocked the front door and reached inside to the rack where she and her mother kept their keys, and she tossed Adolfo the yellow pom-pom to which the Mustang's keys were attached. "Car's in the garage. Pull it around back—I'll be back down in a sec—"

Adolfo did as he was told, loading his folios in the trunk, assessing the space available for his baggage that he'd hauled down to the alleyway behind his sister's garage, awaiting pick up. There would be enough room for it all if Maggie wasn't bringing much—if she had heard him when he'd told her she'd have to leave room for his art supplies because making tattoos was how he was going to support the two of them in Tres Mujeres.

He needn't have worried. Maggie's room consisted of a bed made with military corners, a desk free of clutter—pencils in a wallpapered cup, a bowl of paper clips, a music box her father had given to her for her fourteenth birthday. Except for a rather large math prize—a twelve-inch gold-tone trophy engraved with the formula $E=MC2$, a stack of jazz CDs from Raylon, and the framed marksmanship certificate she'd earned with Raylon's guidance, the room was unadorned, indicative of Maggie's Spartan style. She dropped her backpack on the floor by the desk—right where she would have left it if what she had planned for the weekend was the senior class trip—and yanked one neatly packed yellow duffle bag from the closet. She hoisted the duffle over her shoulder while she retrieved an envelope from the front pocket of the backpack and headed downstairs to her mother's kitchen, where she propped the envelope on the table, between the salt shaker and the pepper. Then Maggie took one last look around and, impulsively, lifted a hand to her mouth and blew a kiss to her childhood.

"Ready to hit the road?" she called to Adolfo as she slipped out the kitchen door and locked it behind her, skipping a step or two on her way to the car. "Ready for an adventure?" she sang.

He didn't know whether it was the skipping or the singing that made him realize how incongruous this scene was—a teenager ditching the last six weeks of high school to go live in a place she'd never been, with a guy she'd known for only three months.

A guy who was living with AIDS.

"Adolfo?"

He shook himself out of his reverie. "Ready." He took the yellow duffle from her and threw it in the trunk.

## Beth

Beth sat at her kitchen table, her hand gripping the stem of her wine glass like a vise, the rest of the bottle sweating on the table, waiting for her next pour. Beside the bottle was a shredded envelope and the card that had been inside, a funny little drugstore card with a cartoon owl on the front and, inside, the message, "Owl be missing you!" under which Maggie had scribbled in her loopy hand, "But I'll have fun this weekend anyway! Jeanine and I drove my car to the school parking lot, so we won't need a ride back on Sunday. See you then! Maggie."

Beth allowed herself to be pleased that Maggie was taking the initiative and starting to drive her own car. And that she had the whole weekend to worry about how she was going to approach Maggie about the Adolfo problem on Monday.

The doorbell rang—Raylon with daffodils in one hand, a bottle of Jameson's in the other. Since leaving work he'd lost the tie and exchanged his khaki pants for jeans. The sleeves of his fresh, white Oxford shirt were rolled to the elbow. "There's a piano in your front yard." he said.

# Maggie

Driving above the cap-rock, between Slayton and Post, the all-night radio played monotonous songs from the eighties, songs that Maggie hated, but she let them play since Adolfo had chosen the station. The songs were so unpleasant that, even if she closed her eyes, the notes were just notes—not colored, not dancing. Adolfo had given up the driver's seat at Abilene and was slumped against the passenger door, eyes closed. Maggie hadn't questioned him when he'd pled exhaustion, even though she knew the events of his day had been trifling, and she knew he was glad for the peace of finally getting away. The road was nothing but a series of long straightaways with no left turns, so Maggie was happy to take her shift at the wheel. The white clouds that raced across a brilliant half-moon were beautiful. She yawned and lowered her window, thinking the night air would keep her awake.

Since leaving Austin, she had been doing calculations in her head—distance driven, distance to go, average speed, all of the relevant statistics in both miles and kilometers. She figured they were nearly halfway to their destination when the outline of Slayton appeared, twinkling lights scattered atop a giant earthen table. A gas flair burned high into the sky. Adolfo raised his head off the window and pointed as they approached the Sands Motel. "All I want is a bed, any bed, as long as it's not at Olivia's and I'm closer to my mountains."

Gravel crunched under the car's tires as Maggie pulled into the parking lot. Adolfo groaned softly as he twisted in his seat to pull a wad of cash out of his hip pocket. She took it and walked the few feet to the office to register.

Maggie had asked for a room on the ground floor, knowing Adolfo was tired, but it was a surprise to her when he put his arms around her waist and leaned heavily on her shoulder, just to make it into the room, and collapsed on the bed.

She said his name, but he didn't answer. She removed his shoes and socks, and his flannel shirt. When she went for his belt buckle to remove his pants, he groaned and rolled onto his side, away from her.

"I'm not a virgin, you know," she said. When he said nothing in reply she added, "And I know how to have safe sex. My mother's lectured me about how to have safe sex for years, and I didn't want to have sex with you just now anyway, I was just trying to make you more comfortable."

He pulled his knees to his chest and his T-shirt rode out of his jeans, exposing the base of his spine, his tattoo, the Virgin's feet perched on a new yellow moon and wrapped in a deep bramble with roses and thorns. The petals were the same violent color as the blood dripping out the puncture wounds in the Virgin's legs.

"Adolfo?" Maggie asked again. She felt his forehead – damp, but not hot, and his breathing was even. She didn't panic. She knew the difference between exhaustion and sickness.

Maggie lay down beside him on the bed, running a finger along the half-moon of tattooed skin that peeked out from his shirt. "For a tattoo artist, you sure don't show yours off," she told him. Again he didn't answer, so she propped herself up on an elbow and carefully peeled his shirt up and over his spine.

"Adolfo!" She was shocked by the awful beauty of what was hidden beneath his clothing. Instead of the usual piously folded hands, the Virgin's arms were outstretched, her palms pleading, her hair and brilliant blue dress blown back as though from a terrible wind. And her face… It was both beautiful and hard. Tears fell from her dark eyes, her sorrowful gaze lifting to the heavens. Maggie was both mesmerized and uneasy. Tentatively she ran her fingers over the Virgin's flowing black hair, over Adolfo's soft, delicate skin. But then she quickly lowered his shirt and curled beside him, troubled, unable to remove the sad, hopeless image from her mind. The Virgin's tears filled her with a wintry dread, following her into a fitful sleep.

# Saturday before
# Palm Sunday,

*April 2004*

## Tilly

**T**illy Anaya stepped out of her *tienda* into the crisp pure air and opened her arms to the warm sunlight streaming through the crack in Tres Mujeres peaks, igniting the frosted windshield of her Jeep Cherokee into a million tiny prisms. She used a long, scarlet fingernail to set the paper clock on the door—"Back in one hour". She used her reflection in the glass door to smooth the vivid purple eyeshadow that highlighted her lustrous black eyes and adjust the thick black braid that lay over her shoulder, ignoring the gray hairs that were lately cropping up among the strands of black at her temples.

The run on beer and frozen burritos wouldn't begin until sometime just before noon. She had time to visit her daughter at the village cemetery, only half a mile away. At Rachel's grave she would offer the same prayers that had for three years gone unanswered, and listen for her daughter's voice from the other side, some clue that would solve the mystery of her child's death, salve her own sorrow. In the time since Rachel's death, Tilly had organized the village women, marched on the *morada,* convinced the brotherhood to reclaim its responsibility as village protectors. It had taken the men six months to get clean, but when they did, they too took up her cause, "No to *chiva!*" With the *hermanos* at their side, the police raids began. Grandmothers along with their granddaughters were jailed for dealing. Husbands and brothers. The Mexican dealers that weren't jailed, fled. Now the overdoses were down, and still Tilly felt no satisfaction. The goddamn *chiva* was still around. People were still dying young from the heroin and the bastards who sold it. And she still did not know why her daughter had to die.

Tilly drove south toward Chimayó, to the small graveyard enclosed by a dry-stacked rock wall on the edge of the canyon rim. The cemetery was a patchwork of white headstones, the earliest of which dated 1690; the quarter acre held the dead from generations of the ten families who'd founded, and still formed, Tres Mujeres.

Beer bottles and candy bar wrappers littered the skid-marked gravel parking area. Piles of blackened road snow had collected along the rock wall, some of them dotted by frozen, beer-yellow patches of urine. Beyond the pine trees, the canyon fell away, a thousand feet of air and scree.

Rachel's grave marker was taller than most, a cross made of wrought iron with filigree around the edges, and it was visible from the road. The cross pieces were united by a glass box, large enough for the 5x7 photograph – Rachel's graduation picture.

Plastic flowers adorned most of the markers. At Rachel's, Tilly placed fresh lilies in the dead grass, then unhooked the tattered green bungee cord that secured a clear glass vase to the cross. She emptied the dead stems and leaves, then carried the vase to the rock wall where she filled it with the cleanest of the road snow. She arranged the flowers in the vase and inhaled. For Tilly, the aroma of the lilies recalled her daughter's tender devotion to this season. The memory of Rachel – her songbird voice raised in praise of the savior who'd died for her, her wet brown eyes, always grateful – would, for the moment, keep Tilly's anger at bay.

Before reattaching the vase, Tilly opened the glass door and removed her daughter's graduation picture. The edges were curled, weathered, but the image of Rachel's beauty had survived. Tilly moistened her handkerchief with road snow and cleaned off the glass.

Rachel had been just eighteen when she died, a few months from graduating as the valedictorian of her class, a good girl who'd avoided the badness that had spread through these mountains beginning in the late 1980s, when Mexican dealers chose the area because of the proximity to the two Interstate highways. Rachel had spent her last afternoon on Earth preparing the *Sanctuario* for Holy Thursday services. This much Tilly knew. What she didn't know, and no one would tell her, was why, on that Wednesday night, Rachel had gone to that trailer, that flophouse. That drug den. The sheriff was able to say only that he'd found her body outside of it, alongside two drug dealers. He could not speak to Tilly's convictions that Rachel had been there only to try to save her older sister, Rita, who loved the *chiva*. He could neither confirm or deny Tilly's assumption that the tattoo artist had also been somehow involved. The Vigil brothers had tried to be helpful by bringing copies of the crime scene photos to her *tienda*. Perhaps, they said to her, if she looked at them she would see a clue that the police had missed, but she had never been able to face the horror in their stack of 8x10 black-and-white pictures.

The wind whipped a white plastic bag caught along the rock wall. Tilly raised the collar of her red wool coat. She knelt by her daughter's grave, damp earth seeping into her knees, and for the next hour, Tilly prayed that the truth of what had happened at that trailer would find its way to her at last.

# Beth

In that instant just before consciousness, Beth caught the smell of bacon, thought that maybe Maggie was downstairs cooking Saturday breakfast, and that today she had little to do but make plans for her daughter's graduation. Then the hangover arrived – mouth parched, headache, muscles that felt as if she'd run a marathon – and the previous night's panorama unfolded. She hurried downstairs careful not to trip over the hem of her oversized Longhorn night shirt.

"You've been asking me to stay over, but this isn't what I had in mind," Raylon said, to the sound of eggs frying. Jeans rumpled and sleeves rolled to his elbows, he pointed the spatula at the coffee pot. "From the look of things, you better have some. Quick."

"I hurt all over," she croaked. "My mouth feels like Brillo. Don't you have a secret remedy?"

"Food or whiskey, take your pick." With a laugh and a shake of his head, Raylon ladled bacon grease over the egg yolks. "I was planning to savor that bottle of Irish all weekend."

"I wish you hadn't brought it," she groaned and sat down at the table, which was set with white placemats and matching napkins and silverware, as well as large glasses of orange juice. Last night's daffodils were revived in a vase at the center of the table. Filtered through Venetian blinds, the morning light was hopeful, like stripes of a rainbow. One sip of her coffee and the reason she'd drunk over three-quarters of a bottle of fine whiskey the night before hit her foggy brain – an image of Maggie in bed with Adolfo.

"She listened in to my health class on STDs," Raylon offered, referring to Adolfo's sister Olivia. He placed a plate in front of her – crisp bacon, rye toast, marmalade, and two perfect eggs. She'd told him one of her life's little pleasures was breaking the yolks of over-easy eggs and watching the yellow flood her plate; he grinned now as he watched her pick up a piece of toast to dip.

Raylon took his own plate from the warming oven and joined her across the table.

"I've got to go see Olivia today."

Raylon nodded, noncommittal, content to let her tell him why before he spoke.

"She doesn't like me, you know. Olivia. She was one of Bill's prayer circle, a groupie." She sipped her coffee. "For a time, I was one of them too," she conceded. "Then Bill's lymphoma relapsed. I couldn't stand the prayer sessions with all that arm-waving, people laying hands on him. Each time he went into remission, at least one of them would say it was because God answered their prayers – as if beating cancer was a competition for God's will." Beth squeezed her eyes. "When I left the group after Bill's second relapse and went back to school to become a nurse practitioner, they all told me I was selfish to do it. But I had to do something. It was clear Bill wouldn't recover. I had to be the bread winner, pure and simple. They wanted me to hold hands with them and sing folk songs around Bill's death bed, as if... if I believed hard enough, God would provide..." She shook her head and ran her hands through her hair. "When the cancer got the upper hand, it was pretty clear they all thought it was my fault, since I had abandoned the prayer group."

Raylon reached across the table for her hand. "You know life doesn't work like that."

"Maybe not," Beth said. "This morning it seems as good an explanation as any other, you know. If I had been a better wife, my husband wouldn't have died." She choked, and coughed. "If I had been a better mother, my teenage daughter wouldn't be dating a twenty-nine-year-old drug addict with AIDs."

Raylon squeezed her arm, knowing it was not the time to contradict her. "Why do you want to see Olivia?"

Beth sat upright and combed her hair with her fingers. "Because, in spite of being a spiritual lunatic, Olivia can also be a practical person. I would like to try to enlist her help with Adolfo, get him to break off with Maggie. I think she might understand that he isn't good for Maggie, and I'd like to have her on my side... when Maggie gets home on Monday and I have to tackle this problem."

Raylon nodded. "I'll go with you."

Beth looked over at him. "Really?"

"That's what friends do," he said, and added, "That's what boyfriends do," and made her grin.

## Adolfo

Clines Corners was a one-gas-station crossroad at the top of the high plains, where Highway 285 crosses Interstate 40 on its way north to Santa Fe and beyond. Adolfo unscrewed the gas cap and stretched his arms, inhaling gas fumes and the mountain air as the fuel pumped. In spite of his five hours at the wheel, he was invigorated by the stiff north wind laced with the sweet smell of piñon smoke.

Maggie was asleep on the back seat, curled under a yellow blanket she'd taken from the motel, using Adolfo's black parka as her pillow. The sight of her and the scent of the mountains made him feel exuberant – up here he'd been somebody, a sought-after artist, a trusted member of the *hermanos*, and he was returning to reclaim his life, with a beautiful girl on his arm.

He re-cradled the pump handle and gasoline splattered off the nozzle, across his silver-toed boot. The boots were black lizard, hand-sewn, with narrow undercut heels and long pointed toes capped with silver, not the kind of boots seen in Texas – these were Mexican boots, flashy. The smell of petrol in the wind ignited memories of his previous life, Tres Mujeres, and his first tattoo shop in a former Sinclair station where, on rainy, winter days, the gasoline odor leached out of the abandoned tanks.

He kicked open the door of the mini-mart. His muscles felt hard – knotted like a boxer's. The attendant behind the counter was a tall man in his sixties with blotched skin that hung loosely off his jaw. "Good morning!" he bellowed at Adolfo. "Don't break my door now!"

Adolfo shoved a crumpled fifty across the counter. The spilled gasoline had dampened the creases of his boot top, so he wiped it against the calf of his black jeans. He held his foot off the floor and admired the sparkle in the polished silver toe.

The attendant handed him his change and Adolfo leaned across the counter to gather it up. "At your age," he said to the old man, "you ought to know who not to fuck with." Adolfo crammed the change into the pocket of his jeans and the attendant backed away, palms raised. Adolfo smiled as he strode back to the car.

For three years he had kept himself hidden in a crummy apartment over his sister's garage in Austin, Texas. He hadn't talked about his dedication to the *hermanos* – hadn't scared his hymn-singing sister or her prayer-group friends with his deeper faith. He hadn't rolled his eyes at the frat boys and bad girls who came to Ruiz's studio to get tattoos of their girlfriend's names on their biceps or a sorority symbol inked on a well-turned ankle without any understanding that tattoos were more than a trendy decoration. They were art – lifetime commitments to art on a living canvas. Up here, faith was hard and sharp like the blades of the yucca rope he'd felt that first Good Friday. Up here, ink – the virgin in all her magnificent, glorious colors – was faith.

In less than a mile his mountains would appear on the horizon. He leaned over the driver's seat of the Mustang and shook Maggie's ankle. "Wake up."

She ran her fingers through her unkempt curls.

"The mountains," he said. "They're coming. Sit up so you can see them."

Groggy with sleep, Maggie gripped the blanket beneath her chin, a yellow cape, and climbed over the console, into the front seat. Adolfo started the engine and, minutes later, the Mustang cleared the rise. The whole panorama of mountains and snow and clouds rose into view. He veered over onto the gravel shoulder and barely took time to cut the engine before jumping out of the car. The cold wind gusted, blowing his hair over his face. A dried tumble weed rattled off the fence line, hitting his leg, disintegrating into tiny branches. He rounded the car and opened the passenger door.

Leaning forward against the north wind, Maggie stepped carefully, stockinged feet against the gravel, to the front of the car.

"Pecos Baldy." Adolfo pointed to the large gray peak that filled the horizon. "Beyond that are the *Tres Mujeres*. After the snow melts, you can see grooves from the glaciers." He reminded himself of a tour guide at a national park, corny with enthusiasm, but didn't care. "For me that's home. It will be the same for you."

She leaned her shoulder against him. Wind whipped the blanket from around her shoulders and Adolfo gathered the wool around her, laying his arm across her shoulders to keep her warm and bundled inside of it. Maggie shivered. She gripped the blanket around her neck with one hand and poked the index finger of the other out, under her chin. "Right up there," she said, pointing at Tres Mujeres. "That's where our new home is, right?"

"Right," Adolfo agreed.

"Right there in that little notch."

## Olivia

Oliva's house was a tidy white frame two-story off Red River near Thirty-eighth Street. An unattached garage with apartment on top was to the right and, on its left, was a small orchard of peach and apple trees in full bloom. Inside, floor-to-ceiling drapes covered the windows of the dimly lit living room. The walls were adorned with banners celebrating Pentecost, Easter, the Eucharist, all but one of them made in workshops at the retreat house on Lake Travis during Bill's glory days – days when Beth had worked extra hours to pay for Maggie's school and tutors. When Bill had become too ill to work full time, the Parish Council had cut his benefits, including the break on school tuition.

In the center of an ornate mantle was a framed 8x10 glossy of Bill's prayer group, Bill surrounded by adoring adults. Beth wasn't one of them. Above it was another banner, this one professionally made in white silk, featuring an image of a stylized child with an opened mouth and hands held head high, with green lettering that said: "Shout it out." The banner was the logo of the renewal movement that had caused Beth and Bill the sort of problems that might have escaped people who simply wanted to share their faith. The charisms and personal Bible interpretations, and the visions and the healings and all that came along with the movement was too much for a cradle Catholic.

"Beth used to call that one the marriage wrecker," Olivia said to Raylon, when she caught him eyeing the banner.

Beth gasped. Olivia's smile told Beth that Bill had let the group in on the details of the marital disagreements Beth had thought were private, between just husband and wife.

"I'll get us coffee. I've just made it fresh. I guess the Lord told me you were coming."

She was dressed in a pleated tan skirt and white blouse, and her limp blond hair was pulled back in a bun. She looked matronly, and too formal for a Saturday morning in her own home, as if she'd been expecting guests. Beth had forgotten about Olivia's glassy-eyed look, the one that let others know she had that special relationship with the Lord. Still, Olivia didn't question why Beth had come to her house on a Saturday morning, bringing the doctor along with her. Maybe she *had* received a special call that visitors were coming.

"I remember you from the health talks you gave at the high school, Raylon," Olivia called from her kitchen. "And, of course, you two work together at the clinic. She placed a ceramic sugar and creamer set, and three china cups and saucers, all with a different pattern, along with a hot glass pot of coffee on a melamine tray and brought them into the living room.

"I've come to talk with you about your brother. Adolfo…" Beth said, and the words made Olivia's hands shake so much as she poured, she had to put the pot back on the tray.

"What has happened to my brother?"

"Well—" Beth frowned, but Raylon understood the cause of Olivia's anxiety immediately.

"Nothing medically, Olivia," he offered.

"Then?"

"He's been seen hanging around the high school," Beth blurted. "With my daughter."

"Oh…!" Olivia exhaled. "That's not right. I'm there every day. Your Maggie and my brother? I don't think so!"

"It doesn't matter what you think, it happens to be true," Beth told her. "It's also true that Adolfo has been talking about leaving Austin, going back to some mountain town in New Mexico – and don't deny it," Beth added when she saw Olivia start to shake her head, "because I'm one of the people he actually talked *to*. I think you should probably encourage him to go but, in the meantime, I'd appreciate it if you would talk to him about how inappropriate it is for a man of nearly thirty to be dating a teenaged girl."

Olivia had raised a trembling hand to her mouth while Beth spoke. Her anger made it difficult to speak. "You don't have to worry about Adolfo," she managed. "He has already left for his mountain town, as you call it. He isn't here anymore to bother your daughter."

# Jimmy

It was late morning when the rig-foreman removed the last of the ten palettes of drill casing from Jimmy's truck. The well site was ten miles south of Levelland, surrounded by miles of irrigated cotton dirt.

"This one's been capped for years," Jake said and hoped off the fork lift. He was a wiry man in his fifties with sunbaked skin and a slick bald head. He'd been around wells long enough to carry authority whenever he spoke of them. "The way prices are going, even these old girls are worth redoing."

A gust of sand-filled wind whipped across the road, and Jimmy turned his head for protection. The surrounding cotton field had been recently plowed and planted. Tito appreciated the neatness of circular rows. In the distance he could hear trucks moving along US 385. Any one of them could be loaded with drugs.

"I'm worried about my rig. The transmission," he said. His next haul wasn't until the following Tuesday, irrigation pipe from Clovis to Denver City. He had a little time and he was fishing for way stations Mexican traffickers might use. The problem with the transmission, real enough, was as good an excuse as any.

"Best transmission man around is Delroy over at Hank's Truck Stop and Motel." Jake pointed to the highway. "Go south 'bout three miles to state road 557, then west toward Muleshoe. Can't miss it."

"Works weekends?" Jimmy remembered the road from his study of the map.

"After church." Jake hitched up his Carhartt overalls. "Best chicken fried steak south of Lubbock."

Jimmy closed the rear gates on his truck. Fifty feet away another gust of wind ripped sand off the cotton row and nearly snatched the way bill from the cab. Jake was still leaning against his fork lift.

"I admire good chicken fried steak," Jimmy said.

Jake handed back the signed bill along with a check. "Don't forget, tomorrow's Palm Sunday. If you're a church goer, Hank's is in walking distance of two. German Catholics to the south. Mennonites to the west."

Jimmy's truck fired on the first try, but it took four attempts before the transmission stayed in gear. "FBI cheapskates," he mumbled as he bumped onto the pavement.

Jimmy found Hank's without a problem – cinderblock compound with six motel rooms, an office and dining room, and a three-stall service area surrounded by plowed dirt. Leaving his motor running, Jimmy began to wander the compound in search of Delroy and noticed a man in coveralls exiting the diner.

"You Delroy?" Jimmy hollered.

The man nodded.

Jimmy explained his issues with the Kenworth.

"I can fix it. Won't start 'til morning after church. Unhook your trailer there on the side then pull the truck into bay number one."

"My next haul begins Tuesday. Clovis."

Delroy was already walking toward a vintage Ford pick-up. "No problem," he yelled back, waving his hand above his head.

## Beth

"You called it perfectly," Raylon told her, steering his Jeep Wrangler one-handed while reading the report of Adolfo's blood work his nurse had emailed to his cell phone. "His T-cells have dropped like a boulder in a plunge pool. The viral load's a rocket."

Beth closed her eyes. She'd avoided the migraine this morning, in spite of drinking so much Irish whiskey it was almost an invitation to the pain, but she could feel the pinpricks again now, behind her eyes, and the throbbing of the veins in her temple that were almost always a prelude.

"Without his medicines – I mean, if you're right that Adolfo has stopped taking his meds – his health will fail very quickly," Raylon continued.

Beth groaned. "If he was on his meds and his virus was controlled, Maggie would be kind of safe. But with no meds and an uncontrolled virus? I'm glad he's gone. I still want to have Maggie tested, though." She rubbed her throbbing temples. "That's the prudent thing to do, right? Have her tested?"

"I'll be damned," Raylon said, pulling up to the curb at Beth's house.

The piano still sat on the front lawn, and Father Tom sat on the piano stool playing it, serenading the neighborhood. He was dressed in his black, short-sleeved collarless shirt and khaki pants, his eyes closed and his bald pate pointed to the heavens.

"Given the chance, he always plays Mozart. Given the neighborhood, it's a good thing everyone's at work or school." Beth pointed to the empty driveways which, in the evenings, held pickup trucks with six tires and American flag decals.

The thick grass was cool against her feet as she made her way across the lawn to Tom. The beautiful notes of his music echoed off the budding pecan tree. His smile was mischievous, defiant, and he pounded the keys with a little more vigor. Beth looked up and down her street, still expecting to see heads peering out the doors.

"Morning, Raylon. So I hear you two went to Olivia's," Tom said, eyes now open. "I got it all from Cecilia." The music changed abruptly to the Simon and Garfunkel song of the same name and Tom belted out a few lines. "Cecilia, you're breaking my heart! Was your visit satisfactory?"

Beth snorted. "I wanted to strangle her."

Tom's hands came to rest atop the ivory keys. "She had no idea her brother was seeing Maggie. He'd talked about returning to that mountain town, but nothing was settled. The truth of it? Adolfo told her very little."

Beth leaned against the piano. "Don't take up for her." She kicked off her sandals and let the St. Augustine grass tickle her toes.

"How did Maggie hook up with this bugger any-way? Cecelia said he has a Virgin Mother tattoo that goes from his shoulders to his waist."

"Our Lady of Guadalupe. I'm used to seeing tattoos on our clients – and when I do, I go on with the exam without a word. But when I first saw this one, I gasped. No piety in his Virgin. Her arms are outstretched and her face is pulled back in fright like she's pleading with the devil."

Father Tom launched into the first few bars of "Devil with a Blue Dress On" and Raylon laughed. "I'm glad you two are having fun," Beth told them, laughing herself. "They met at Whole Foods."

"She worked in produce, he worked the deli," Raylon added.

"A match made heaven," Father Tom declared and played a few more bars of Little Richard. "Fine instrument. We've got to get this out of your yard before it rains." Tom let go with the intro to Beethoven's ninth. "I wonder if it was like this in eighteenth-century Vienna. Saturday morning concerts on the lawn?"

"You better call whomever to finish the job."

"I've called Steve, the groundskeeper. He can bring folding chairs from the parish hall. We'll charge admission to raise money for the school."

"Tom!"

"The truth is, Beth, I came to ask if we could move it back into your house, just for another night or two."

Beth frowned. "You don't want the piano?"

"We *do* want the piano," Father Tom told her. "But there's been a small mix-up – I want to put the piano in the high school's rehearsal hall, but the principal, unbeknownst to me, is taking advantage of the kids being away on the class trip. With so many of the cars cleared out anyway, you know, he had the school parking lot repaved and the new asphalt isn't cured yet, so we can't drive the truck up to the door—"

The heat in Beth's temples was immediate. The explosion in them followed before she could bring her hands to her head, as if she was trying to contain the fallout.

"What?" Father Tom asked.

"I need to go to the high school right now," she said.

"Sure…" Raylon agreed.

"Put the damned piano wherever you want it, Tom. Raylon, please, *now*," she cried as she ran back to his car.

## Maggie

Snowflakes swirled like dust devils among the adobe houses as Adolfo parked in the gravel lot of Dave's, a small restaurant in a blue-collar area not far from Santa Fe's historic square with its high-end shops and Native American craftsmen.

Maggie jumped out of the Mustang and twirled in the midst of the falling snow. "So this is it, the famous Dave's." She laughed, her voice fresh, ready for singing. Her flannel shirt, unbuttoned, hung open over her tight-fitting olive T-shirt and the ends flapped as she danced. She reached for Adolfo's hands and circled him, dancing a two-step. "This air does smell like heaven."

Her dance had charmed him so that his impatience with her had vanished. The glass panel door to the restaurant was steamed over. "Welcome to the first of my places," he said as he pushed it open for her.

Except for the lone workman wearing a green Baca Electric cap, the lunch crowd had gone. Adolfo chose a small table along the back wall for them, beneath a large black-and-white photograph of a Cuban girl, dirty and clothed in rags, standing at the entry to a tin lean-to, staring north across the Caribbean. Cuban jazz played on the stereo, and the air inside the small diner smelled of onions and red chiles. Maggie let go of Adolfo's hand and jerked a thumb toward the restroom sign, offering him a grin before she skipped toward it. When she returned, she slid into the seat opposite him, tossed her flannel shirt onto the adjacent chair, and started to tap her fingers on the table to the beat of the music.

"You are happy?" Adolfo asked.

"So very happy," she said, and she let her body begin to move with the music. She extended her arms to him. "I'm so glad to be out of that car. Dance with me."

Adolfo liked it that she was a good dancer – and even better, he liked that her T-shirt had ridden out of her low-slung corduroys.

She pointed to the speaker. "Tito Puente. Come on… dance with me." Her voice was playful, almost mocking.

Over her shoulder, the waitress, a thin woman with spiked black hair, studied them from behind the counter. Adolfo squinted at her, and she glared back at him, but Maggie didn't notice the exchange.

"Come on," Maggie said again. "Nobody's around and that waitress won't mind."

Adolfo shook his head, then scooted his chair flush against the wall. "I don't dance."

Maggie merely shrugged at his rejection, continuing to keep time to the Latin rhythm, slowly rising from her chair. The tight white skin of her belly moved back and forth like an invitation. She held her arms above her head, moving in a slow circle, the T-shirt riding even higher.

Adolfo knew what she was really asking him to do. Until now, he'd dreaded her expectations, but since he'd seen the mountains? The closer he got to home, the better he felt – perhaps tonight he wouldn't disappoint Maggie yet again.

When the song ended, the electrician, who was now at the door, buttoning his coat, gave a whistle and a clap. Maggie turned to him and bowed, one hand on her stomach, the other behind her back. Adolfo's face grew hot. "Whistle at your own damn woman!" he yelled, but the electrician replied with a laugh and was out the door.

"It's only dancing," Maggie reminded him.

"Dancing so everybody can see." He pushed her chair out from under the table with his foot. "Sit down. I'm ready to eat."

But she didn't obey. She stepped closer, and with her knees pressed against his, she tucked her T-shirt into her corduroys.

"Stop that. Stop it. Sit down so we can order."

Maggie started to laugh again, then checked herself. She'd thought he was blushing at her attempts at seduction, but even she could see the heat in his face was anger. She plopped down on the chair he'd shoved out for her, looked down at the table and plucked a lock of her hair to twist around her finger. Adolfo sat back in his chair, as far away from her as the table allowed.

"Fifty-six more miles," she said. "I've kept track in my head the whole way. Three hundred and thirty-seven miles since last night. The Sands Motel was ten miles from being halfway."

"How do you do that?" Adolfo asked in real wonder, propping his elbows on the table.

The waitress approached their table, near enough for Adolfo to see the small tattoo on her shoulder – a Japanese chop.

"Strength," he said aloud. Chops had been the craze back then, girls in their twenties wanting an exotic foreign symbol. "Strength," he repeated, and raised a fist, but the waitress still didn't respond, so he ordered two green chile cheeseburgers with fries. He wanted something serious to drink, but they still had two hours of driving ahead of them, so he ordered ice water.

The waitress kept her eyes on the small green pad, nodding as she scribbled their order but, before she walked away, she said to him, "I figured I'd never see you again."

Adolfo looked up at her then – really looked at her face for the first time. Her chop had been his last work of art before he had awakened in the hospital. Today the young woman looked much older than he remembered. The lines in her face had deepened and her skin, so smooth and brown back then, was sallow. Her spiky black hair-do was a far cry from the waves of lustrous chestnut brown hair that had once hung below her shoulders.

"Rita," he said.

Rita nodded and, without sparing another word for him or a glance at Maggie, she hitched her hip against the swinging Dutch door into the waitress station, turned and disappeared into the kitchen.

# Adolfo

Two sisters, both beautiful. Rachel had been his girlfriend. Rita had been into the smack. Now one was dead and the other looked like the girls that came to the clinic.

Adolfo didn't acknowledge her as she placed their plates on the table. It was enough that she'd seen him, seen that he was still alive. He had abandoned Tres Mujeres. Now he was back, to take his rightful place once again. This was enough. For now. He waited until she'd retreated before he picked up two French fries and bit into them. "Try them," he urged Maggie. "The best fries in New Mexico."

Maggie twisted an errant lock of hair and turned her head toward the photograph. Like the Cuban girl, her look was far away.

"Or don't try them, I don't care."

Maggie ducked her head and continued to work the misplaced curl.

He watched carefully. It irritated him that he felt he had to suck up to his girlfriend, entertain her because she was being sullen. That Rita would see her being bad-tempered with him and tell that mother of hers. When Maggie dropped the lock of hair she'd been worrying, he relaxed. For the moment, she was back to normal – no dancing, no showing off, no putting his decisions up for discussion. Then she bit into her burger and immediately reached for her water.

"Hot. Hot. Hot," she panted and fanned her mouth even as she coughed and tears streamed out her eyes.

Adolfo broke off a piece of bun and lathered it with honey from a squeeze bottle that sat on the table along with the other traditional condiments. "Eat the honey," he said, holding the bun out to her.

Maggie grabbed the food from his hand and choked it down.

"Better?" he asked when she'd stopped coughing.

Maggie took another long slurp of her water before she spoke. "How do you know that waitress?"

Tito's. Holy Week, three years ago. He'd had a fever all day and he hadn't felt well enough to work, but Rita had insisted. She wanted her tattoo right now, and it was such a small one. Surely he could manage just a small tattoo for her? He'd just finished Rita's chop when Rachel arrived. And the shooting started. He remembered running into the forest behind Tito's trailer to hide, but he had no idea how he'd gotten to the hospital in Española.

"Everything fine here?" Rita asked, just like any waitress in any diner asking any table if their food was satisfactory. Then she turned to Maggie. "Sweetie, you've hooked up with a bad one." She fumbled in the front pocket of her black polyester apron and tossed Maggie a slip of paper. "With him, life will get hard, fast. Call me when it does." Then she was gone, back into the kitchen.

That he had not received a hero's welcome from the first familiar face he'd seen made his head ache with confusion. And his stomach knot with fear.

"I'm finished." Maggie pushed her plate to the center of the table. The music changed. Maggie pointed to the sound. "Ibrahim Ferrer."

He wanted to shout: I survived! I wasn't killed by those rampaging drug dealers! I am here, I am back! I am home!

He wanted to tear up Rita's piece of paper, but it was gone, along with Maggie. All he saw was the door to the ladies' room slam behind her.

Rita walked over to the table and slapped the bill in front of him, a pale green piece of paper torn from her small pad. Adolfo grabbed her wrist and held it on the table top. "I'm home, Rita. I'm so happy to be home."

Rita jerked her arm free of his grasp. "I'm really sorry to hear that. Because my sister's not coming home."

Adolfo frowned. "So I heard."

Rita cocked her head, silently asking for an explanation.

"I was back in Austin. Tito called, inviting me to use his trailer. That's when I learned."

As a measure of restraint Rita hid her clenched fist behind her back. "She's dead, asshole, and all you can say is 'So I heard'?"

## Tilly

Bands of snow showers fell in Tres Mujeres. The weather made for a slow day at the register, so Tilly reorganized her display shelves, making room for the order of dry goods that had arrived on Friday – mops and chamois cloths, and a dozen plastic buckets. Women in Tres Mujeres believed in spring cleaning, and Tilly had all the supplies they would need. When the phone rang, she leaned a cardboard rubber glove display against the end of an aisle and went behind the counter to answer it.

"Mom," Rita said, her voice hesitant.

"Rita?" It was always a surprise when her daughter called. Since Rachel's death, they tread lightly around each other. Tilly knew of Rita's sickness, but her daughter had given it to herself, sharing needles with creeps like that tattoo artist. At least she'd had the courtesy to move away, down to Santa Fe, so her mother didn't have to watch her grow weak.

"He's back," Rita said.

Tilly knew whom she meant.

"In the restaurant. Today. With a pretty girl the same age as Rachel."

Tilly recalled her graveside prayer and wondered if the return of this scarecrow was God's answer.

"He's driving a red Mustang."

Adolfo's chair and transfer machine were in Tilly's storeroom. She knew he'd come around soon enough to claim them.

"He said he didn't remember details about Rachel."

Tilly struck the counter with her fist at the idea of it – that her daughter's murder was too insignificant to remember.

"I'm sorry for this girl. I gave her my phone number for when she gets into trouble."

"More help than you gave to your—" Tilly stopped herself.

"Than I gave to my sister," Rita supplied, but Tilly had already hung up the phone.


## Maggie

After Chimayó, the road climbed steeply into black and gray clouds. When the rear tires fishtailed on shining black asphalt, Adolfo hollered, "*Chinga*," bouncing his palms off the steering wheel.

Maggie tightened her seat belt and wrapped her arms round herself. Adolfo was unrecognizable, and there was this odd rhythm to his speech. If he weren't driving, Maggie thought, he would be shadow-boxing, his body keeping time with his words. She'd never before seen him angry. If she needed to take Adolfo to the hospital, how could she drive this road alone? She felt like a pipe swing in a school yard: one side was the thrill of it, the other was danger.

A break in the clouds brought a brief patch of blue sky. Maggie wiped the fog from her window, enough to see the steep canyon falling away from her side of the road. She gripped the armrest as if to hold the car away from the ledge, then counted the white crosses planted along the roadside – two, three, four – all decorated with plastic flowers. As they passed the clustered memorials, she reached for the motel blanket in the back seat.

Then the road abruptly flattened. Adolfo slowed the car to a crawl and pointed out the passenger window, to a one-time Sinclair station, now a small *tienda* selling beer and pop and groceries. "My first shop," he said, grinning like a child at his birthday party. The fruit bins beneath the portal were empty; pieces of cardboard filled the missing panes in the service bay door. Adolfo craned his neck as if expecting a Welcome Home banner.

The road forked, and while most of the village stayed off to her right – a collection of store fronts and compacted houses, all with thin curls of smoke rising for their chimneys – Adolfo veered left. As he passed a small wood-ramed church, pieces of sunshine penetrated the low-lying clouds and sparkled off the wet black pavement. He cracked his window and inhaled. Beyond the church, he took a dirt road into the trees, driving another quarter mile and stopping at last in a grove of Ponderosa pine. "What do you think?" he asked, spreading his arms on either side of the steering wheel, at the thirty-foot Airstream in front of them.

"This is it?" Maggie gasped.

The trailer, dinged and spattered with mud, was at least forty years old. It was supported by cinder blocks instead of tires, the side panels were heavily rusted, and the undercarriage clogged with dead branches and plastic grocery bags.

*I feel like the girl in that photograph in the diner*, Maggie thought, envisioning herself in rags, staring out into the distance from the doorway of the hovel before her.

"Our own little nest in the middle of the National Forest. When the wind blows, little pine cones drop down, like somebody's throwing rocks or something on the roof. I'm warning you so you don't get scared."

Maggie remained silent, taking in her new home.

"What's the matter? Are you too good for a house on wheels?"

Maggie shook her head. "It doesn't even have wheels," she cried. "It's an old, abandoned piece of junk in the middle of nowhere, and it doesn't even have wheels!"

Blood rose to Adolfo's face. "This is my friend Tito's place. Me and him, we're close. Like this." He twisted index and middle fingers together and jabbed them in the air. "Stuck like glue. He doesn't like to be in the snow, so in the winter he goes to El Paso. So his place is empty. Straighten up, *mujer*."

"You've asked him if we can use it?"

The deadfall scraping the underside of the Airstream sounded like boney fingers on a chalkboard. With each gust of wind, the screen door banged against the siding.

In truth, Adolfo hadn't spoken with Tito for two years. And the last time he'd seen the inside of the trailer, it was a piece of shit in there too.

"It's free." He grabbed his parka and jumped out of the car and ran toward the trailer. Maggie sat alone in the Mustang, the engine running, the warm air blowing on her feet, afraid to follow him inside.

## Adolfo

Like a child returning home to his treasures, Adolfo stepped eagerly into the trailer. Except for a few standard built-ins – a small table with a bench on either side of it, and a bed frame that held a thin, stained mattress – the trailer was empty. The soft leather cushions, fake Tiffany lamps, and

Navajo blankets that were etched in his shaky memory were long gone. Layers of dirt and discarded plastic bags covered the floor. Clusters of small crosses made of peeling duct tape were on the walls, five on each side, a new addition. Adolfo wondered how long the trailer had been abandoned.

His shop had been at the *tienda*, but during the final year of his life here in Tres Mujeres, this trailer was where he'd worked and lived. People came by at all hours – some for tattoos, some just to talk, others strung out needing to crash. Now he would bring this place back to life.

He kicked a plastic bag and saw the stain on the floor. The red-brown color was unmistakably blood. Beneath the duct tape he knew he would find bullet holes, five shots fired from the outside. That much he remembered; there had been five shots in all.

Adolfo pulled the mattress off the bed frame onto the floor to cover the stain. Then he went to the door, tightened his jaw, and motioned for Maggie to come in.

Maggie was startled by his look – eyes hooded, his lips pressed in a down-turned line. She assumed he was angry with her for not mirroring his excitement. Outside, snowflakes, helpless in the wind, tumbled across the hood. She hesitated before she turned off the ignition, put the keys in her pants pocket and grabbed the yellow blanket for warmth.

"What do you think?" he said with his arms extended, welcoming her in through the battered door. Before she could answer, he said, "This is good, right? This is good. Damn."

The smell hit her as she crossed the threshold. The smile on his face no longer made him look handsome to her. It made him look foolish. The expression on her face told him she thought he was a fool.

"When you said Jimmy's place at the edge of the National Forest, I thought you meant it was a log cabin. A cabin in the woods, with a fireplace and one of those braided rugs. My Uncle Steve's Winnebago that he takes on hunting trips is better than this." She was reluctant to breathe in the foul air, and her voice sounded thready.

"With a little clean-up, it'll be good. You'll like it, I promise. We have a table and a place to sit." He pointed to the circular bench built into the front wall of the trailer. "And some pans and utensils." He rattled the array of knives and forks in the single drawer next to the sink that refused to close all the way. "And even a refrigerator."

When he opened the door to the small unit under the counter beside the sink, she saw the origin of the sour smell – a carton of half and half with mold growing up the sides, a packet of hot dogs that looked as if they had grown fur, a plastic bag that might once have been chicken parts but was now an oozing, gelatinous pool. She raised her palm as if to block the odor. "This is not what I imagined."

Adolfo slammed the refrigerator door. "Life is adjustments. Grow up."

He stepped closer to her, and Maggie wondered, for a split second, if he would block her exit if she tried to leave.

Then, without thinking, she jerked the car keys out of her pocket and bolted back to her car, the yellow blanket trailing like a cape. She started the engine and slammed the Mustang into gear. Unaccustomed to its power, she spun gravel on her way back to the paved road. Her tears started as she rounded the small white-frame church, and they flowed as she raced to the town. She slid to a stop in the parking lot of the *tienda*, leaving a long, swooping 'J' in the layer of gathering snow. Her tears had started small, but as she cut the engine, her sobs had grown to a flood. She dropped her forehead against the steering wheel, trembling, dripping snot onto the yellow blanket.

She was unsure exactly why she was crying. Fear for what she'd done – leaving her home to live in a foul-smelling, decrepit old trailer in the middle of nowhere. Guilt for leaving Adolfo – how could she abandon him with a storm coming, no heat or lights or food, his medicines in the trunk of the car. Failure to be anything but a naïve little girl who set out to change her life without asking questions, making plans, thinking things through. She lowered the back of her car seat and pulled the yellow blanket more tightly around herself. Perhaps this was just what she deserved, to sleep alone in a cold car.

## Beth

The back of her skull hummed like a speed boat. Her brain felt like bowling pins after a strike. She and Raylon had driven to the high school, driving in ever larger concentric circles on the streets surrounding it, looking for Maggie's red Mustang, until it became clear to them both that the car, and Maggie, were gone. And Beth began to weep with the pain.

Her first migraine had arrived the day of her senior prom, the week after her mother, who'd been an upstanding citizen in their small community, the president of a local Savings and Loan, ran away with the bank's accountant. The scandal had included embezzlement as well as infidelity.

The evening of her prom, she and her father had an argument over her prom dress. It had been purchased for her by her mother, from an exclusive Dallas boutique, and it reminded her of the shame her mother had so recently brought upon their family. "I don't need her expensive dress," Beth said when her father asked her why she wasn't wearing it. "I'll wear something else and we can return it next time we go into the city."

What her father understood her to say was that she didn't want to spend his limited resources on a fancy dress, now that the two of them had to get by without her mother's good salary. "I'll not have my daughter going out in rags," he'd bellowed in reply.

In the end, Beth skipped the prom altogether. The paralysis lasted twelve hours, the blinding pain and nausea for three days. Her father stayed with her in the hospital room, missing whole days of planting to be by her side. Hemiplegic migraine was the official diagnosis. Beth just referred to them as *The Headaches*.

Using the wall for support, she now edged herself into the house and up the stairs to the bathroom, where the waves of nausea turned projectile. Her vomit fell between the toilet and the tub. Raylon reached for the light switch, losing his grip on her arm, and she tumbled onto the cold tile.

"Just let me lie here," she gasped, as Raylon tried to help her back to her feet. He nodded, pulled a clean towel from a shelf, rolled it and placed it under her neck.

Her most recent attack had been almost two years ago, on the night before Bill's funeral. After the rosary, the prayer group had come back to Beth's house for what they called fellowship. Beth called it free food for the inconsiderate. Raylon had been among the last to leave. Despite her heroic efforts to remain upright, she collapsed before he'd cleared the front door. The last word she'd said before becoming mute was "migraine," and he understood. He carried her up the stairs and slept right there in the bedside chair.

The next morning, he awoke early, at Beth's pained whisper for a glass of water. He ran into Maggie in the hallway on his way to the kitchen. His stammering attempts at an explanation made him—and Beth—seem only more guilty.

Raylon bent now, moving slowly and soundlessly around her as he mopped the floor with paper towels. She tried to push herself into a sitting position but the nausea returned and she threw herself over the toilet, vomit splashing into the water.

"You need to rest, Beth." Raylon wiped her mouth with a fresh towel.

Beth squinted her eyes against the bathroom's dim overhead light. "I need to find Maggie," she croaked.

"Tomorrow, Beth."

"I need to find Maggie," she repeated, sinking again to the floor.

"Let me get you into bed—"

"No—" The cold tiles were a relief under her burning scalp. She shivered and curled herself into a fetal position, her head under the sink and her legs curled around the base of the toilet. "I need to find Maggie," she sobbed. "Why would she do this? Leave with that awful man? I need to find Olivia, find where they went, find out where they went... What is the name of the town…"

"Tomorrow." Raylon brought a pillow from the bed, tucked it under her head, and draped a blanket over her shoulders.

## Maggie

Maggie was startled by a quick tap on the window, followed by the car door being opened and a beautiful woman motioning to her. She was an older woman, and her black eyes shone with sadness and the offer of safety. Snowflakes stuck to the woman's long braid. "Honey, come inside," she said.

Cold and coatless, wrapped in the yellow blanket, Maggie trudged behind her in the now-ankle-deep snow.

Inside the little store, the woman shook the melting snow off her lumberman jacket, then turned to Maggie. "I'm Tilly." She gestured around the *tienda*. "This is my business." Shelves were lined neatly with canned goods, boxes of pasta and rice, candies and breads. Mops and buckets and other cleaning supplies were in a corner to the right of the narrow check-out counter, and a tall, glass-doored freezer with frozen foods was to the left. The low ceiling was supported by wooden logs, *vigas*, running lengthwise. Warmth radiated from a potbellied stove behind the counter, and a cast iron teapot rested on top.

"Maggie." She extended her hand. The woman's grip was rough and firm, and welcoming.

"Honey, you need to dress for up here," Tilly said, taking Maggie's yellow blanket and hanging it alongside her own on hooks behind the counter. She reached for two mugs on a shelf over the cash register and filled them with black tea from the teapot. "Drink this," she said, as if the tea was the true remedy for girls lost in a storm.

"Thank you." Maggie held the mug with both hands, warming them.

Tilly took her cup over to the stove where there were two rattan chairs. "Join me," she said.

Maggie seemed disinclined to speak, so Tilly carried the conversation. She spoke slowly, soothingly. "For two generations this was a Sinclair station. My father and his father before him ran it. A few years before Poppa died, a big company built a fancy station at the bottom of the hill, so I started making tamales and sold them along with candies and pop, *biscochitos*, *chicharróns*." Tilly shrugged. "When Poppa died, I shut down the gas pumps and turned this into a *tienda*."

Maggie had been absorbed by the *latillas*—counting the number of nails in each, then the number of nails in the ceiling total... The woman spoke carefully, as if she were telling a bedtime story, but something in her cadence, so similar to Adolfo's, made Maggie feel what she was saying was but a prelude, and she was nervous to hear the whole tale.

"You have a pretty car," Tilly said and sipped from her cup.

Maggie turned from her counting, the comforting, colorful numbers filling her head. "It was a birthday present."

"Your car, then?" And when Maggie nodded, Tilly added, "I wondered where Adolfo would get himself such a car."

Maggie thought she would spill her tea. "You know Adolfo?"

Tilly pointed to crisp black lines of a spider web tattooed on her neck. Maggie recalled what Adolfo had told her, that for a while his shop had been in the service bay of this old gas station.

"Of course!" Maggie cried, feeling a spark of hope she thought had been doused. "You're who we have to talk to about getting Adolfo's transfer machine and other stuff so he can set up his shop. We've just moved here to

Tres Mujeres, just today, and Adolfo's going to set up his tattoo business again —"

"Where?"

Maggie didn't like the suspicion in Tilly's voice.

"He took you to Jimmy Montaño's, didn't he? That shit-hole for drug dealers and dope fiends out in the woods?"

Maggie's eyes filled with fresh tears, and she lowered them as she lifted her mug to take a sip and hide behind it. It shamed her that Tilly would know exactly where she and Adolfo were setting up their life together.

"Tonight, you're staying with me," Tilly said.

Tilly lived in a two-bedroom doublewide on a cement foundation connected to the *tienda* by an enclosed walkway. The furniture was wood composition covered with black Naugahyde, the countertops pale yellow Formica. The dull-green shag carpet was flat, as if it had been stepped on for generations. But the tortillas and the bowl of green chili stew Tilly fed her were delicious. The hot bath she drew for her was soothing, and the old flannel nightgown she gave her to put on was warm and smelled lovely.

## Adolfo

Adolfo was surprised by how deep the snow had become around the trailer in just a few hours. He was surprised too by the discomfort he felt, and not just from the cold that seeped into the trailer from under the floorboards and through the loose seams. He was surprised how much he missed Maggie—the way she broke into a dance whenever music filled her head, and the way she filled the air with chatter, even when he didn't feel like talking. He knew she couldn't have gone far, not in this weather, but he was surprised at how frustrated he felt that he had no way to know how far. How anguished he was that he didn't know if she was safe.

Adolfo zipped his down parka around him and braved the snowy cold, going first to the power switch on the outside meter, then to the gauge on the propane tank that was buried behind the trailer. The five-hundred-gallon tank was half full. He turned his head to the heavens and gave thanks. Then he opened the valve and returned to the house, where he lit the pilots on the heater and stove.

He hadn't known what to expect of this old trailer. Though he never would have told Maggie, he'd been surprised it was in as good a shape as it was. It had been a crime scene—that much he knew—but by the time the bullets had begun to fly, he'd been on his way to weeks of fever dreams in the hospital. Why couldn't he remember more. Even being found alone on the highway—another homeless junkie dying of chiva or AIDS or exposure—was only a fog-ridden memory. He'd been found far enough away from the trailer that no one had connected him to the drug dealers shooting it out in the clearing around the Airstream.

Now, he supposed, the old crime scene belonged to him; if Tito ever showed up, he'd be happy to share, of course, as Tito had once shared. The ease with which he was settling into the old place—remembering exactly where the outside meter was located—made him feel a sense of ownership.

And then he remembered.

Adolfo dropped to his knees and crawled to the closet opposite the sink. He shoved open the door and pulled out his pocket knife to use the blade to pop the weather stripping—but the plywood backing, a fake back that opened to a compartment behind, had already been pulled away. Back in the old days Tito had used this hiding place for a variety of contraband—drugs, mostly. Adolfo reached into the darkness and lifted out the contents—scales, a roll of plastic baggies. He turned on his back to extend his reach and groped around in the compartment. He had nearly decided it was empty when his hand landed on—he jerked his fingers away. Vermin? But he had felt nothing like fur, and there was no stench of something dead... He reached back and pulled out a dozen bills, all hundreds, neatly folded and secured with a paper clip. Over a grand. The hiding hole had clearly already been uncovered since the last time he'd tucked something secret away, and he marveled that whoever had searched it had missed the money.

But he was the lucky finder. He and Maggie were set now until he could get his equipment and start making art again. If, that was, Maggie hadn't left him completely— turned her back on him and her car back onto the road to Austin. Given her reluctance to drive and the darkness of the night and the snow continuing to fall, however, he didn't think she would have attempted such a trip.

He rifled the bills, almost happy. And then he *remembered*.

He stumbled out the door of the trailer, down the steps, into the snowy woods. He followed no trail, and on any other night his parka would not have been warm enough, but he felt no cold. He did not find the stone under the Douglas fir; the stone found him.

It took him an hour to roll the stone away and dig far enough beneath it. His fingertips bled before he came to the oblong ammunition box. What he found inside it weakened him. Four one-kilo blocks of Mexican black tar heroin, uncut and tightly wrapped in clear plastic with a red mark on the underside; ten thousand dollars in cash, rolled and secured with a rubber band; and a heavy 9mm semi-automatic pistol. He released the twelve clip; only seven bullets remained.

He didn't know if he was lucky because he'd found a windfall of ten thousand dollars, or cursed because he'd found a gun. Or a dead man because he'd found a fortune in heroin with a street value of over two hundred thousand dollars that some dealer or another was in all probability out there holding a grudge about.

He stood up, staggering in the lightly falling snow, and vomited into a snowdrift until all that was left inside him was acid bile. He wiped his mouth on the sleeve of his parka and brushed the snow from his shoulders. Then he fell to his knees and curled his head into his hands, laying down in the surprisingly warm and comforting snow, longing for sleep.

He dreamed of the day three years ago, when he had awakened early in preparation for his upcoming role as Jesus in the Good Friday procession. He'd been clean for a week—not that he'd ever used daily, but whenever there was a party, he didn't hesitate to join in. He never thought it odd that the men he saw sober at the *morada* were the same men who came around to the trailer at midnight strung out and looking for a fix. All of it was part of the same mystery. It was those very men who'd encouraged him to stay clean for his Good Friday re-enactment.

He dreamed that he'd begun to cough, and by the time he went to the *tienda* to use his transfer machine, to print out the Japanese chop selected by Rita, his chest felt wrapped in adhesive tape. When he returned to the trailer at noon, his legs were rubber. Still he'd made the Good Friday practice at four that afternoon.

Spring had come late that year, so the ground in the meadow was a bog, and the snow bank on the north wall of the *morada* reached almost to the roof. Beyond the *morada* was the trail for the procession, with markers for each of the thirteen stations. Three hundred yards beyond the building, in the clearing at the top of the trail, three crosses leaned akimbo. The way he felt, he doubted he could carry himself up there, much less make the trek with a heavy cross on his shoulder. The Vigil brothers had driven nails into the cross beam—for the weight they'd said, but Adolfo knew their true purpose was to rip at his skin.

The dream ended abruptly, and Adolfo realized it had been a memory, too.

# Maggie

Shortly after midnight, Maggie was awakened by clattering out in the store, a crash of tin cans.

"Where is she? Where is Maggie? Her car is here and she must be here, too!" Adolfo spilled words out in Spanish so that Maggie understood only her own name.

Tilly shouted back at him in a voice clear and cold as the night air. "How could you come back here? And bring another girl to ruin, to my house!"

"Shut up, old woman," Adolfo shouted, slurring his words. The sound was followed by the scrape—metal against wood.

"I'm calling the police." Maggie heard Tilly's threat, followed by Adolfo's laugh.

"Now our police are different," she screamed. "They're tough. They want our village clean. So you get out—you're not wanted here."

"Hand me the fuckin' keys," Adolfo demanded, but by then Maggie had made it to the store, her bare feet cold on the tile. She held up the too-long nightgown with one clenched fist, the other shielding her eyes from the store's too-bright lights. She had never seen Adolfo drunk before. The sight of him staggering, his black puffy coat partially zipped and covered with dirt, made her gasp. "Did you *walk* here?"

His black eyes were narrowed, rat like, as he wobbled toward her. "I did, Maggie, my woman! And now I'm cold! Drive me home." He extended his arm and flicked his fingers. Maggie moved to steady him, but Tilly blocked her way. She struggled against Tilly's arm. "But he's sick. Look at him."

"You're not giving him the keys to your car, and you're certainly not going anywhere with him." Tilly flicked her head toward the bar across the street. "If he got himself to Claudio's, he can get himself back to the trailer."

"Maggie," Adolfo whined, but his eyes suddenly became unfocused. He reached for her, teetered, and collapsed, his head just missing the potbellied stove.

Maggie pushed against Tilly's arm, but Tilly held her still. "He's sick," Maggie cried.

"Sick, hell. He's drunk."

Maggie relaxed in Tilly's arm. "I know," she said. She stood with Tilly amidst the wreckage of Adolfo's visit—a shelf of Campbell's soup cans rolling on the floor, a display of Cap'n Crunch cereal crushed underfoot. "But he's sick too, Tilly," Maggie whispered.

Tilly sighed. "The virus. Like the common cold around here."

Maggie blinked in wonder at the flatness of Tilly's acknowledgment. "I haven't seen him take any of his pills today. And he couldn't have taken any tonight because they're in the car, and I ran away with the car…"

Tilly started to pick up cans and re-stack them on the shelves. "He came here on Easter break from art school, twenty years old and innocent, and walked the Good Friday procession. For some people, that first time is too powerful. Word was that the stripes on Adolfo's back bled for a week."

Tilly motioned for Maggie to pick up a few cans that had rolled her way, and the two of them resumed the restocking. "He left after that, for almost twelve months. Then he came back. Stayed for six years. He was charming, baby-faced, and an artist with the tattoo gun. Still is, I guess. Back then nobody could stay away." She pointed to her neck. "I should've known better."

"Why be guilty over a tattoo?" Maggie asked.

Tillie shrugged. "Up here, everybody's guilty of something. God and the *chiva*, that's why they fit together so well."

# Palm Sunday,

*April, 2004*

## Beth

Beth walked slowly through the empty sanctuary in search of Tom. The church still seemed filled with the triumphant, bittersweet music of Palm Sunday, though the celebration of the day's first Mass was complete. Father Tom was in the sacristy, a room infused with the odors of candle wax and incense, folding his vestments and placing them in a wide, shallow drawer. He picked his black coat off the side chair, then motioned for her to follow him back through the sanctuary. Their footsteps echoed off the marble floor up to the oak trusses of the vaulted ceiling. In the vestibule, Tom turned off the lights, all but the single spot over the altar.

When Tom pushed open the large wooden door to the outside, Beth was momentarily blinded by the blast of morning sun and failed to see Olivia standing there on the church steps among a few stragglers. Her normally tightly pulled bun had feathered, and her tight smile appeared forced more than it usually did.

"He is my brother," Olivia said as Beth and Tom approached. She stretched her hand to turn over to them the piece of yellow paper she held in it.

"She's my daughter," Beth said, swiping the paper, not kindly, from Olivia's fingers. "He's thirty years old and he's taken my eighteen-year-old daughter and run away with her. He's a thirty-year-old man with AIDs and he's kidnapped my daughter—"

"Beth," Tom said, a priestly inflection in his voice, Beth thought, calling for calm and reason, and it made tears spring to her eyes.

Olivia could only nod, the confidence that God's will was being done now gone, in this time of crisis. "I'm sorry. But there's more."

Beth knew what was coming. "His pills?" Abruptly, she sat on the church steps.

"I found them on the shelf in his bathroom, but I don't understand. Why did he stop?" Olivia pleaded, as if Beth would surely have the answer.

Beth looked up at the two of them standing over her. "Because they weren't working anyway." She didn't say it to be unkind; kindness, simple kindness, in this case, was the simple truth.

Olivia slumped beside Beth on the church steps, hands clutched in her lap. Moments passed before the women could look at each other.

"What if he's gone back to the drugs." Olivia lowered her head. "That's the true reason he left Austin."

Beth shivered in the spring heat. In a way, Adolfo's return to heroin made sense to her—stopping his anti-virals and going back to the heroin, waiting for the disease to take him. She'd seen it happen before.

Father Tom squeezed Beth's shoulder, to steady her. She stared at the stone step beneath her feet. The yellow piece of paper slipped from her fingers. Olivia bent and picked it back up, held it out to Beth. "I've written it here."

Beth took the paper as if she'd never seen it before.

"It's all there, as much as I know. Where I believe Adolfo has gone. I don't have an address, just the name of the town, and a map to show you where to go when you get there."

Beth's shivers crawled up the back of her neck, humming like a power boat, then worked down her arm so that the paper shook in her fingers. She was glad for Tom's steady hand, still resting on her shoulder. "Thank you, Olivia." She turned her head to the woman who had been her enemy, knowing that they both had someone to lose if she didn't pull herself together. "Thank you."

## Adolfo

Adolfo awakened before the others. Despite his drinking and a night on the floor, he wasn't sweaty or nauseated, and his mind was clear and sharp like the sun streaming through the polished glass in the door. The smell of piñon didn't fade as he warmed his hands on the iron stove. Even his mouth tasted fresh, untainted by the nasty pills. He folded the blanket Tilly had draped over him at Maggie's insistence and placed it on the counter. Before stepping outside, he grabbed the yellow blanket off the wall hook. Ravens cawed in the windy pine boughs. Fortunetellers, he thought, but he would not presume to know what they foretold.

He was hungry. He walked out the front door of the *tienda*, careful to hold the little alert bell still with his hand. He tossed the yellow blanket into the Mustang, then walked through the shin-deep snow the half mile to Lupita's, a small metal hut with a drive-up window, a revamped snow cone stand, the town's best and only breakfast place. He recognized Lupita's daughter, Nichole, who was just a gangly child when he'd last seen her. Back then she loved teasing him and Rachel about their romance, reciting a childhood taunt—"Adolfo and Rachel, up in a tree, K. I. S. S. I. N. G!"—and had giggled uncontrollably when he'd teased her back—"Nichole's in the school yard, what shall we do? Send her to live with the old woman in the shoe."

"Two bacon and cheese burritos," he told her, then flashed a smile, waiting for her to remember him.

Nichole rubbed a bit of sleep out of her eyes to stare at her first customer of the day, and called his order to her father in the back of the hut. Adolfo laughed to himself, taking a seat at the short counter where customers waited for their orders to be filled before taking them away, sitting in full view of the sleepy girl as she filled napkin holders and the bins for salt and pepper packets. He relished the moment when she would realize who she was serving. A few minutes later she handed him a paper sack containing his food, and he slid a ten-dollar bill across the counter toward her. As she slid his change back to him, and looked up to give a good customer a grudging early morning smile, he caught her eye, and she stared at him for a moment. Then her eyes widened with surprise.

"Nice to see you," Adolfo laughed.

Nichole didn't answer. She darted her eyes to the floor and backed toward the kitchen and the safety of her father.

"Nice to see you," Adolfo insisted, still laughing, and Nichole returned a grimace that Adolfo saw as the shy smile of a young adolescent. "See you around, kid." He grinned as he walked out the door of the hut.

The cold air had lost its punch, leaving in its wake a promise of snow-melt and apple blossoms. Adolfo side-hopped a mud hole. His mouth watered at the smell of red chile and bacon in his bag. He'd gone for years without food like this in Austin. Without his pills he had a ferocious appetite, and a lot of eating to make up for.

A dust devil whipped a filthy paper plate and a crumpled napkin across the *tienda* parking lot as he crossed the street to eat his food and wait for Maggie to wake up and drive them home.

# Maggie

Maggie awoke to find a fresh set of clothes—brown corduroys, a red wool shirt and patterned socks, even underclothes, folded on the bedside chair. A puffy black parka similar to Adolfo's hung from the back of it. Out the bedroom window of Tilly's little home, she saw Adolfo sitting on the hood of her car in the parking lot, hungrily eating a burrito. Part of her was annoyed with him for assuming she would walk out of Tilly's door and return to the trailer with him. But the larger part of her felt utterly happy that someone in the world depended on her for care and affection. The word *love* slipped through her mind and she gasped with surprise. Watching him through the window, she played with the possibility of it.

"Adolfo and Maggie. Love, lovers," she whispered, then giggled to herself, wondering if she had truly arrived at that blessed state—a place she once thought impossible given her oddities. Her heart pounded, her body was overheated. She thought she should run to him and spill the news, but decided to dwell in the feeling alone until she was sure.

Instead, she showered and washed her hair, and donned the clothing Tilly had laid out for her. She found a pink plastic, old-fashioned vanity set on top of the dresser and picked up the brush to tidy her hair. Just in front of the vanity mirror was a framed photo of two pretty girls, both with long, straight black hair. The younger one was wearing a long white dress with puffed sleeves and an elaborate lace collar. Beside it was a paper fan stamped with the words, "Rachel's Quinceañera". Maggie had attended several such celebrations for friends in Austin, but what was more immediately on her mind was the older girl in the picture—how familiar she looked. She squinted, trying to figure out who it was she looked like, but at last simply shook her head: the girl looked like Tilly, who was clearly her mother. She replaced the pink brush on the dresser and turned away before her mind could latch onto that other niggling thought: *Who did Tilly look like? Why did she look so familiar?*

Inside the empty *tienda,* Maggie collected a few items she needed if she was going to make the trailer livable: a mop and a bucket, bottles of generic window cleaner and toilet scrub, PineSol, a container of Comet, and a box of scrubbing sponges. By the time Tilly entered the shop for the day, Maggie had calculated the cost of her purchases, figured the applicable tax, and counted out the exact change, which she handed to Tilly.

Tilly sighed with disappointment—all the supplies Maggie had chosen meant that she had a house to clean. Adolfo's house. Tito's house. That filthy drug den. "Forty-four dollars and twenty-three cents?" Tilly snapped. "We'll see." She proceeded to ring up the items on the cash register and was astounded that Maggie had hit the amount to the penny.

"It's kind of a gift," Maggie admitted, gathering up her cleaning fluids to carry them in the bucket and tucking the mop under her arm. "Thank you for everything, Tilly. I'll bring these clothes back as soon as I've been able to wash them—"

"No, no. Wait!" Tilly insisted as Maggie turned toward the door.

Maggie paused.

"I mean," Tilly stammered, "I mean I thought, it's Palm Sunday, you and I could go to the ten-thirty Mass together. The Sanctuario is so beautiful, and we can go early because you'll want to take pictures. Here!" Tilly turned to a shelf behind the cash register and grabbed a disposable camera from the small display. "See, we can take pictures! Then, I thought, we could go to lunch—"

Maggie smiled even as she shook her head. "Getting away from the churchy people back home is one of the reasons I'm here. Going to Palm Sunday Mass isn't something I'm interested in doing. But thank you. Thank you for everything," she repeated and, when Tilly again pursed her lips to protest, Maggie said, firmly but kindly, "I decided to finish what I started. Adolfo needs me— And I think... I think—" She turned the phrase, *I think I may love him*, over in her mind, and it was such an unusual and novel idea that she didn't see the subtle signs that would have alerted her to the growing fury that was overtaking Tilly.

"I gave you a clean bed, and good food, and I offered you friendship and protected you from that man when he crashed in here drunk in the middle of the night! You can't return my kindness and go with me to Mass?" Her voice rose with each syllable until she was shrieking. "How can you go back to that indecent place with that man who murdered my daughter!"

Maggie stepped back as if she had been struck. Holding the pile of her dirty clothes as a breastplate with one hand, the bucket and mop with the other, Maggie backed up toward the door.

"Go!" Tilly screamed at her. "Go, then! You'll never be anything but another lost little girl!"

Maggie reached the door and struggled to juggle her burdens so she could open it. "And you're nothing but a crazy old woman!" she shouted back to Tilly as she fled.

# Beth

The drive from Austin to Lubbock took six hours, but Beth knew the back roads, short cuts around the towns, and long, straight two-lanes made perfectly for speeding. Little about these byways had changed since Beth had belonged to them. Driving west, the borrow ditches traded bluebonnets for Johnson grass. Oak trees vanished into mesquite. The smell of it reminded her of high-school cowboy, Billy Wayne, the same guy Raylon had competed against, riding saddled broncs. She smiled at the memories of her summer before college—car sex beneath drilling rigs, empty beer bottles tossed into open slush pits, skinny-dipping in her father's stock pond. A different world then, she allowed; Maggie's world would never be so innocent.

Five hours into her six-hour trek, Beth's car was akimbo on the side of a two-lane, modestly paved road, smoke billowing from the engine. Beth raised the hood and, hearing the *thunk thunk* sound of boiling radiator water, she figured immediately the issue was a broken water pump. The car had lost its first one at 40,000 miles and she knew better than to touch the radiator cap.

To her recollection, Hank's, an out-of-the-way service station and repair shop, was not far up this very road. Hank had once leased cotton land from her dad, though surely the old man himself was long gone at this point. Still, she had no choice but to walk west and see if the old place was still in business.

She'd walked about three-quarters of a mile, lost in the aromas of Johnson grass and fresh-plowed earth, when she was startled by the call, "You lost? Name's Delroy," Delroy drawled in his thick, West Texas accent, as Beth gasped and regained her composure.

"Beth," she returned the greeting. "My car's broken down a bit up the road. It's the water pump."

Delroy shot a line of spit through the match head gap between his two front teeth. "You go to the doctor and tell him what's wrong with you before he examines the ailin' part?"

Beth started again, and then she laughed. "Go see for yourself," she told him, digging the Subaru's keys out of her purse and tossing them to him. "The only thing is, I'm in a hurry to get to Santa Fe. I need it fixed yesterday."

Delroy sauntered to the wrecker. "If it's the water pump, it'll take me about twenty minutes to fix. Should get you outta here sometime around noon tomorrow."

"Well…" Beth stopped on her way into Hank's small convenience store. "That doesn't make any sense. Why can't I leave today if it's going to take you only twenty minutes to fix the pump? You've got plenty of time."

"Lady, time I've got, parts I don't."

"I'll pay extra."

"Extra for what? Parts gotta come from Lubbock and, Ma'am, it's Sunday."

"But I'm needed in Tres Mujeres," Beth whined. "Can't you send somebody to pick the part up? Or rent a car to me and I'll go get it myself. Just tell me where."

Delroy shook his head and pointed to the office. "Who do you think's going to be in on a Sunday in Lubbock either? You just sit yourself down. Single room's fifty a night," Delroy said and shot another stream of spit.

In her desperation, Beth used her last ace. "Where's Hank?" she demanded.

Delroy laughed. "Gone to Cabo for honeymoon number six. He assures me this is the one." Delroy pointed to the motel. "Get yourself a room while I fetch your car." Beth was so taken aback that Hank was still walking this earth—let alone spry enough to take on another partner to walk with him—that she simply obeyed.

Beth carried her embroidered suitcase inside the small convenience store and paid a bored teenage boy for an avocado green, cinder-block room for the night, and picked up a pint of Jack Daniel's. The single window in her room was plugged by an air conditioning unit that blew hot air, and she could get no reception for her cell. She figured she might as well be out in the heat of the day, so she gathered a handful of change from the bottom of her purse and walked to the pay phone that was bolted to the outside wall of the motel three doors down.

"Raylon."

She heard him sigh, equal parts frustration and relief. "I asked you to wait until Watson returned from vacation so I could drive with you."

Not wanting to respond to the idea that she waited until Wednesday to start off on this mission, she asked, "Are you still on rounds?"

"Yes, as a matter of fact—"

"Well, I'm almost halfway to Santa Fe right now. I couldn't wait, Raylon."

"Clearly."

"Are we going to fight about this?"

Raylon let her simmer for a couple of moments, but he didn't want to be cruel. "No."

"Good. Look, my car has a broken water pump. I'm at an out-of-the-way truck stop motel not far from where I grew up—" Her voice hit a high note as she was startled by a small brown lizard that crawled from behind the pay phone into the crease of sunlight on the avocado wall.

"Wait for me there," he said. "I'll pick you up as soon as Watson returns."

"Raylon…" She sighed. "My car will be ready tomorrow." The lizard had relaxed into a spot of sun and she found its ease infuriating. She flicked her index finger and it fell to the ground. For a moment it seemed as dazed as she felt. Horrified that she'd done such a vicious thing, she watched as the lizard looked side to side for the malicious finger. "It's God's finger," she said aloud. "He's doing to me what I'm doing to you." The lizard seemed to understand and scampered toward the parking lot.

"Who are you talking to?"

"A lizard."

"A *lizard*?"

"A green and brown lizard that was sunning itself on the cinderblock at this crappy motel I had to check into. I thumped it."

"Not Billy Wayne?"

"Stop the joking," she said. While Raylon was still laughing, she untwisted the cap on her Jack Daniel's. "At least they sell liquor at this godforsaken place."

# Adolfo

The sun radiated off the silver walls like a forgotten happiness. This was how he had wanted life to be: living in his mountains, free of drugs—*all* drugs, especially the anti-virals that were supposed to keep him well but made him so sick—Maggie with him, inside, happily cleaning and making the trailer their home. The sight of her walking out of the *tienda* carrying a mop and a bucket with all sorts of soaps and solutions stuffed inside had made his heart so glad it had ached inside his chest. She was coming home with him!

Even so, even though she was coming back to the trailer with him, there had been only the thinnest veneer of happiness in her about it. She had climbed into the passenger seat of her car, throwing her cleaning supplies in the backseat and telling him he'd have to drive, and where she wanted him to drive first was to the closest Walmart. She wanted clean sheets and blankets and pillows and towels, she'd told him; she hadn't asked, this had been a demand. While she was in housewares, she said, his job was to go buy a braided rug—a multi-colored one like she had envisioned back when she'd assumed Tito's was a mountain cabin.

He had given her her way without complaint, even grateful for her demands if it meant she was coming home with him, but she didn't seem to appreciate it.

It was the Vigil brothers, he decided, who'd done this to her, soured her and spoiled what should have been his joy in his homecoming, and this day of homemaking. They'd met up with them in the Walmart parking lot as they were loading the Mustang's trunk with Maggie's bags of sheets and towels, along with the braided rug he'd purchased.

"See, there," Adolfo had said to Maggie, pointing to three young people, none of them older than fifteen, maybe sixteen, crowded around the cart return slot, around a short, muscular Mexican with close-cropped hair wearing a blue parka much too heavy for a day that was warming quickly, melting the previous evening's snow into a memory. "It's a deal going down," he'd told her, craning his neck for a better look. "Marijuana—no question about that. Too clean for *chiva*. Too casual for meth."

Maggie shot him a deep frown. "In a Walmart parking lot?"

He'd laughed at her. "Of course. People from Santa Fe, the Reservations, the north, someone's always trying to score something, and there is no more central place to meet up."

She'd been annoyed that he'd laughed at her, as if he were punctuating her middle-class, white-girl naiveté, but her emotion turned quickly—to what? Anger? Fear? Confusion?—as the orange and black county sheriff's car, a Ford Galaxy, eased behind them, blocking the Mustang into the stall where they were still loading Maggie's many purchases.

"The *vato's* come home for redemption," said Aurelio Vigil, the driver.

"Three years. He thinks no one will remember what he did," said his brother Joachim. And then he licked the thin mustache he wore on his upper lip.

Adolfo's thoughts went immediately to the stash behind the closet wall in the Airstream, the riches under the rock. "Banditos," he said, bumping fists, first with Joachim, and then, leaning into the cruiser, Aurelio. "The famous brothers Vigil, with the fast car that knew every little road from Chimayó to Trampas. Why are you dressed like this? You're trying to steal the dope from all the tennis shoes." Adolfo nodded toward the youngsters at the shopping cart stall.

Aurelio pointed to the .38 holstered at his waist. "We're the law now, Tattoo Man."

"You're the foxes." Adolfo laughed again, less easily, Maggie noted, and he pointed to Joachim's mouth, his now-absent gold cap. "You get too broke and sell your savings account?"

Joachim pointed to the patch on his sleeve. "Dental insurance. Rio Arriba County. Besides, the sheriff's department couldn't have us looking like the thugs we were trying to catch."

"Who's the whitey?" Aurelio nodded to Maggie who'd kept herself busy unloading their cart. "She doesn't look like your usual party-bitch to me."

"Neither did the Rachel girl," Joachim added. "He goes for these goodie-two-shoes types, our Adolfo."

Adolfo glanced back at Maggie, who was now bent into the back seat, as if in the midst of loading yet another bag of her purchases, still as a statue.

"Word is out, Adolfo… you and whitey living up in the pine trees in Tito's place," Joachim warned.

"Last guys he let use it, we busted the first week," Aurelio added. Adolfo noticed the bulk of his biceps stretched the fabric of the brown uniform. "Don't be thinking you got something to sell."

"Only my art," Adolfo replied, though Maggie flinched as if she'd heard a catch in his voice. A hesitation.

Joachim reached out of the cruiser and popped his fist against the back panel of the Mustang. "We'll be seeing you," he said as Aurelio drove away, slowly unblocking their exit. Then, just as Adolfo was beginning to feel the relief of their leaving, and Maggie was beginning to unfold and reanimate, Aurelio stepped on the brake. "Tattoo man?"

Adolfo looked up.

"One way or another, we collect our debts," Joachim called. He let the threat hang in the air before both he and his brother burst out laughing. Aurelio peeled the car away, through the parking lot, a fast and reckless show that would have gotten anyone other than police officers arrested.

"Rachel," Maggie said when they were gone.

Adolfo shrugged. "My old girlfriend. You knew I had girlfriends before you, right?"

"The girl that died. Rita's sister."

"I had nothing to do with it."

Maggie shuddered. "Tilly says…"

"What?" When she was silent, he spat, "Tilly says *what*?" He was a hero returned and so far, from Rita to Tilly to the brothers Vigil, he had been welcomed home like an infestation of cockroaches. "*What* does Tilly say?" he'd insisted, but Maggie just wept.

# Beth

Beth filled her ice bucket at the machine at the end of the porch and returned to her room. She placed two cubes in a plastic cup, along with three fingers of whiskey, and pulled the green desk chair outside to watch the sun drop beneath the cotton field.

"God," she said out loud, "why are you doing this?" Frustration had replaced the joy of the road, but her upbringing in the church made her ask herself, *Where is the lesson here? Why am I on this journey? What am I supposed to learn?*

She never considered that the journey was Maggie's, not hers.

She did not consider that she was already on her own journey, one that had begun when she'd been Maggie's age, when she and Billy Wayne had made their own getaway traveling the rodeo circuit through the Texas panhandle into Oklahoma. They'd stayed away for almost two months and returned only with enough time for Beth to pack and head off for Boston College. On their way home, Billy's pick-up had cracked a block not half a mile from this very station, and when Beth called home for help, her daddy had answered, "I'm tired from moving irrigation pipe. Guess I'll fetch you in the morning."

She imagined her daddy cussing it up now with his heavenly friends: "Be careful what ya sow," he'd be saying, laughing and shaking his head that both Beth and his granddaughter had inherited their runnin' shoes from his ex-wife.

By the time Beth had drained her plastic glass, the sun had disappeared, leaving a purple hue above a black line. Clouds of blackbirds lifted off the plowed field into a windbreak of Siberian elms. Beth's disquiet had fallen prey to the whiskey. For the moment, her worry was limited to the water pump.

## Adolfo

By the time they had finished with Maggie's list of errands and got back to the trailer, the sun had slipped beneath the western treetops, striping the trailer-clearing with shadows alternating with golden light, and the night chill had begun. In their absence, two cardboard boxes had been left on the trailer steps. The first box contained a can of Folger's and an electric coffee maker, two boxes of shredded wheat, cans of beans and chiles, rice, strawberry jam, peanut butter, and two dozen fresh tortillas wrapped in tin foil, still warm to the touch. The second was filled with milk, butter, eggs and bread, two rolls of paper towels, and a message written on a sheet torn from a Big Chief tablet: *A few things to get you started. Keep the clothes. Tilly.*

"I figured she wasn't done with you," he said, glaring down at the boxes. Maggie offered him the note, but he backed away as if it were contagious and hoisted the heavier of the two boxes to his shoulder to carry it inside.

Maggie didn't follow him. She sat herself on the bottom step, just enough in the way that Adolfo had to step over the second box backwards to get out of the trailer, pick it up and carry it inside.

"Are you done talking to me? For the whole night? For our whole lives?" he shouted, but even he understood it wasn't that Maggie wouldn't talk to him, it was that she wasn't yet physically able to speak of Tilly's daughter.

Adolfo joined Maggie on the trailer steps. He had cared for Rachel, he explained to her. Not as much as she had cared for him, he suspected, but they'd had fun together, and he certainly wouldn't have harmed her. Maggie was quick to tell him that she didn't believe what Tilly said—that he'd been responsible for her daughter's death. What stunned her as that Adolfo had never told about Rachel's death in the first place.

But for Adolfo it was all so vague. He supposed that was because Olivia hustled him out of the hospital and off to Austin before he could gather up the loose threads of his life, but he could not say even this to Maggie, offer even this much of an explanation without feeling somehow obligated to tell her about the contents of the hiding hole in the closet. What he had stashed there. He could not say these things to her without confessing how very much he did and did not know about how his life here in Tres Mujeres had ended, or how much danger they might both be in.

# Maggie

Adolfo covered the built-in table with the oil cloth from Walmart. Maggie was touched by his effort to make this place right for her. She warmed a can of beans and served them with four of the warm tortillas. So they ate their first simple meal in their new home.

Outside, the sky had reached complete darkness, no alpenglow, the full moon had yet to clear *Mujeres* peaks. The low-voltage ceiling bulbs made the room close, small, and the dim light made the skin on Aldolfo's face look yellow, the bags beneath his eyes a darker gray. One of the duct-tape crosses beneath the window hung by a thread. She ripped it away then squatted for a better look. The hole was the size of her little finger. Its jagged edges singed. *Bullet holes*, she thought. Raylon had taught her to shoot so she had a reference for what she believed she was looking at, and her agile mind had already begun to make a connection between these holes and the dark stain she'd found beneath their thin mattress when she'd scrubbed the trailer, but the thoughts vanished and she stood quickly when Adolfo asked what she thought she was doing.

"You look sick," Maggie deflected. "Have you taken your pills tonight?"

"I didn't bring them," he replied.

Maggie gasped with alarm. "You just stopped them, all of them, on your own?" Suddenly her purpose became a question.

"No. No," Adolfo told her, not certain why he was lying to her. Or if he was lying. "No, the doc said it was OK, like since I was moving I could restart them up here once I got settled. It's just temporary. There's a clinic in Española. I even talked with your mom about it."

"But it's your medicines that keep you well."

"Don't worry. We can check out that clinic next week."

Maggie felt uncertain, but she nodded anyway. Her father had acted in a similar way—he'd had bottles of medicines for pain and preventive antibiotics, and one day he just threw them into the garbage disposal. He believed that if he was just tough enough, determined to get through today and then tomorrow and tomorrow without giving in, the cancer wouldn't catch up with him. "God will heal me without them," he'd said. Maggie had thought him courageous. Her mother had thought him foolish. Maggie worried that without the medicines, Adolfo might no longer need her.

Or, that, like her father, he would die.

After repositioning the bed over the braided rug, Maggie made up the dusty mattress with a new pad and fresh sheets and Adolfo curled into it the moment she'd smoothed the bright, flower-printed Walmart comforter over it.

An hour later she followed him, her ear buds in her ears and the sounds of John Coltrane still soothing her. After midnight, Maggie was awakened by the deep-throated sound of a car engine idling in the clearing outside, and a small stream of headlights pierced the hole that was once covered by duct tape.

# Monday, Holy Week,

*April, 2004*

## Tilly

O n the night of Rachel's murder, the *teinda* had been closed. Rachel had been in Chimayó helping the nuns prepare the church for Holy Thursday, and Rita had been at work in the restaurant in Santa Fe. Both her girls had plans and told her not to hold dinner, so Tilly was busy with a display of gourmet chocolates. Lent was ending and the whole mountain would be running for the sweets. She was lamenting that she hadn't ordered more milk chocolate caramels when Ike Chavez, the Rio Arriba County Sheriff, knocked on her door.

"I'm sorry to intrude," Ike said, standing before her with his cap in his bony fingers, his voice raspy and thick with a spring cold. "There's been some trouble up the road—"

Tilly knew "up the road" meant the trailer, and "trouble" probably referred to Rita. "I can't bail her out again, Ike. She chose this life, the *chiva*. I think the greatest favor I could do her would be to let her pay for her choices—"

"It isn't Rita, Tilly," Ike said.

What she had done then still surprised Ike. Her purpose, and the speed with which she executed it, still made him shake his head with astonishment. She grabbed her plaid wool coat from its hook behind the cash register and her keys from its pocket and brushed past him so quickly that she was in her car and out of the parking lot almost before he could get his cap back on his head.

The moon was full. The pavement glowed a silver ribbon that Tilly followed to the dirt lane, where light flooded the clearing like it was a holiday parking lot. The line of cars facing the trailer with their brights on included three police cruisers, the Vigils' '72 Bonneville with a jacked up rear end, and a rusted Ford van with *Sinaloa* plates. Rita's pick-up was nowhere in sight; Rachel's Jeep was parked at the far end of the clearing.

"Tilly, I wish you wouldn't—" Ike slammed his car into park and jumped out of it to intercept her, but she had already pushed past the people, the police officers and the Vigil brothers, and was looking at the three body bags laid out on the ground by the trailer's steps. When Ike thought about what happened next—and this was something he thought about often—he was still stunned by it. Tilly fell to her knees beside the body bag that held her younger daughter, and carefully and quickly unzipped it to behold Rachel's face—gray and blue, lips parted, drying blood filling the dimple in her left cheek. The pink-and-green print cotton blouse she was wearing had turned maroon where her blood had spilled from the wounds in her chest—two holes, both clean; two bullets in and out of her young, thin body.

Ike, his officers, the coroner, even the Vigil brothers moved to try to pull her away, but Tilly lay down on her side, next to Rachel, the meadow grass cool against her face, and that was where she stayed for over an hour, until her sobs were spent. But her rage was fully formed now And she began to growl, low at first, primitive, her volume growing with her agony, shaking treetops, awakening birds. When she had used all her voice, the meadow became silent, and the Vigils took her home.

"I don't know why Rachel was there," Aurelio said.

"Or what she was doing with those drug dealers," Joachim added. "The other two people who were killed, they were drug dealers. But the police didn't find any drugs inside the trailer at all."

Aurelio was driving and kept his eyes straight ahead when he spoke. "All I can think, there must have been a third dealer who shot up the place to keep the money and dope for himself."

Tilly let them talk. Their words offered her neither comfort nor disquiet. Ever since that night, however, they had turned a new leaf, taken her under their wings, entered the police academy, stopped by the *tienda* almost every day to eat her food and tell her about their progress at their new line of work. By the first anniversary of Rachel's death, they'd become deputies.

# Adolfo

The clearing had been churned by tire tracks. Adolfo stood in circles of twisted meadow grass and stared at the word – *MUERTE* – spray-painted in big black and red letters on the side of the trailer.

His impulse was to berate Maggie for not waking him when she heard the noises of the vandals in the middle of the night. In truth, he faulted himself for sleeping through it all. Back in the day, such warnings were accompanied by burned-out trailers, drug dens smoldering, one dealer finishing off another. In most cases the victors were the brothers Vigil.

Adolfo's impulse was to dismiss the damage. "Just some *pendejos* jerking with us. Don't worry about it," he said as he reentered the trailer. "It isn't meant for us personally."

But he did take it personally. If this gigantic *MUERTE* on the trailer was meant as a warning for him, who had put it there? Who had not wanted him to come home? Who did not want him to become a part of Tres Mujeres again, and why?

He thought of the ammo box. He did not know whose drugs were in there – the only dealer he'd ever done business with was Tito, and never in the quantity that was in the box now. The Vigils, on the other hand, would do business with anyone – meaning they weren't picky about the dealers they intimidated and ripped off or killed to get their drugs and make a higher profit. Were the drugs and the money in the ammo box theirs?

Adolfo shook his head – it was a ridiculous question with too many answers to offer any solution. If the heroin was theirs, how did it get to be buried under that rock? And why were they still looking for it, now that they were the law?

And how had he known to find his way to the rock, unless he was the one who had buried the Vigil brothers' drugs beneath it.

"Adolfo?" Maggie asked and, again, alarmed now, "Adolfo!" He brushed her away and made his way across the meadow to vomit in peace.

## Tilly

Sparrows and chickadees fluttered in the trees at the far end of the graveyard. Coyotes yipped in the distance. A lone dog returned the bark. White plastic grocery bags, hung up on shrubbery and shredded in the weather, waved in the wind. Tilly knelt before her daughter's filagreed cross, released the small bungee cord that secured the glass vase and replaced the bouquet with fresh lilies. She hadn't been back to that awful trailer until yesterday. Taking the provisions there for Maggie had been– What? An act of penance? Of desperation? Trying to save one young girl from Adolfo because she had not been able to save her own?

The ground beneath her knees had become soft from her years of near-daily visits, but today it was uncomfortable. Tilly wondered if she might ever find comfort again after what she'd seen at the trailer. She had always assumed that Rachel had died outside of it, where Tilly had seen her spread out on the ground. That Rachel had gone to Tito's trailer to plead with her older sister not to do the *chiva*, to come home and be good, as she was good, and that she'd been caught in the drug dealer's crossfire. But when Tilly found herself alone at the trailer, she could not simply leave the groceries on its steps as she had planned. She tested the door and it was unlocked, so she let herself inside. Once there, she opened every door, pulled out every drawer, hunting for a thing she could not have named. She kicked the filthy mattress aside when all she could find was battered flatware and a bean pot, and a yellow blanket folded neatly in a cubby. But beneath the mattress she'd found the blood stain and she knew, as she believed any mother would, that it was Rachel's blood.

With trembling fingers, Tilly brushed the dirt off her knees and hurried back to her car. She drove too fast along the curving roads, back to the *tienda*, where she dialed the café where Rita worked.

"Are you busy?" Her voice quivered when Rita picked up.

"Not really." Rita was suspicious – rightly, Tilly thought. For three years she had blamed Rita for her sister's death. For three years her anger had sat between them, heavy and unwieldy, like a fifty-pound bag of pinto beans.

"It was never your fault, was it?" Tilly asked.

Rita sighed. "She loved Adolfo. She never did drugs, nothing like that, but she loved him."

"But how could she love someone like that, all wasted and nasty!"

"Mama, you forget. He was handsome and strong." Rita paused before adding, "Beautiful, like daddy."

Tilly balanced herself against the counter. She hadn't forgotten her own attraction to beautiful men. When she was eighteen, she fell into crazy love with Fidel, her long-ago husband. Adolfo had the same black opal eyes, the same soft skin, the same muscular shoulders.

"Mama?"

When Tilly didn't reply, Rita continued, "Rachel? She was pregnant. She and I had talked and she asked me to be there when she told Adolfo. That's why we were at the trailer together that night."

Tilly felt her knees buckling and she lowered herself to the floor.

"Mama, did you hear what I said?"

Tilly sat beneath the register, her legs sprawled awkwardly under the cigarette display. The receiver swung on its twisted cord and she heard Rita's pleading, "Answer me. Mama, answer me. Mama? Do you hear me?"

Tilly wanted to answer, but she could not yet form words, and then the door of the *tienda* opened.

"Hello? Tilly? Anybody here?" Maggie called.

# Adolfo

Sunlight bounced through the pine trees like a mid-day strobe. Adolfo circled back north, past Tito's, toward the *morada*, which had, more than any other place he had ever known, been his home.

Fresh wheel marks highlighted the two-track lane through the trees. From the top of the meadow, the L-shaped adobe building glowed orange. Several pickups and a squad car were parked along the north side. Some men were rebuilding the trail behind the building, others were resetting the crosses atop the hill. Freddy Rincon, the mayor of the morada, wasn't among them. The large wooden entry door was cracked open and, inside, where Aldolfo knew the air smelled of wood smoke and candle wax, were the *hermanos*, his brothers – the Vigils among them. Not one of them had offered him welcome.

Adolfo stopped short, not parking, letting the car idle by the side of the road where he could see and not be seen. "I'm not here for trouble," he would have told them if he had dared to make himself known; Maggie was right, they were not safe, and that was because he held the Vigils' possessions, given to him on the night that Rachel died.

Beautiful Rachel, who had tasted of spearmint. She had come to Tito's with her sister, but she hadn't come for the *chiva*. He'd been aware of her, even on the first night they'd met, watching him like a portrait artist studying her subject. Beautiful Rachel who loved him, and who he had not loved. The good girl who had gotten caught in the crossfire; the sweet girl who he had not loved.

A murder of crows picking gravel off the car path flushed, their noises echoing in the trees. Adolfo put Maggie's car into reverse and left the *morada* before any of his brothers could notice he was there.

## Maggie

The *tienda* seemed abandoned. No lights and the wood stove was cold. Then she heard a soft sigh coming from behind the counter. "Tilly?"

Palms flat atop the counter for support, Tilly lifted herself to her feet and shook her head.

"What's happened?"

"Nothing," Tilly told her, bending to retrieve the receiver. Before she could cradle it she saw the question in Maggie's eyes and handed it over to her.

"I'll pay," Maggie said, and Tilly nodded, uninterested.

"Use it if you need to make a call," she said and stumbled toward her doublewide.

"OOH-LA-LA," Jeanine said as soon as she heard Maggie's voice.

Suddenly Maggie didn't know what to say. How to tell Jeanine that her cozy cabin in the woods was actually a moldy trailer with a blood stain on the floor, beneath the mattress where she and Adolfo slept. That someone had spray-painted the word *Muerte* on the side of the trailer in the dead of their first night there. That Adolfo had stopped taking his meds and, in Maggie's experience, this meant that, like her father, he was starting to prepare to die.

She needn't have worried. Jeanine filled the silence. "Things are locked down around here, Maggie... I mean closed up like a prison. Your mom discovered where you are and I've been trying to track what's going on since then from whatever I can gather when the grown-ups talk. She's on her way to try to find you, but then I heard her car broke down somewhere in West Texas."

Maggie was so quiet Jeanine thought she'd lost the call. "Maggie?"

"Shit," Maggie replied.

# Tilly

Facing the mirror above the bathroom sink, she examined the delicate spider web on her neck. "Am I that hard?" she whispered to herself, thinking that she must be. She had all but cast one daughter out of her life, blaming her for the death of her younger sister – a girl who hadn't been able to tell her own mother that she was going to have a baby.

Tilly had been the first of Adolfo's one-nighters, all older women caught up by the beautiful new boy and the decorations he pricked into their skin. But that had been well before he got into the *chiva*, when he had been strong and healthy. And vigorous. She thought of the way he had effortlessly lifted her so she could wrap her legs around his waist. How he'd spread his legs into a warrior's stance to bear her weight and allow her to writhe on him as if he were a statue. How, after she had sighed with satisfaction, he'd thrown her on the bed to have his own pleasure.

But now in her vision he wasn't throwing her. It was Rachel he was tossing onto the mattress.

Tilly turned on the hot water and lathered a wash cloth. She scrubbed her neck hard enough to bring blood.

The spider web remained.

## Beth

Beth gagged and choked. The local water made coffee taste like grease and metal. She had forgotten how much sugar it took to make the stuff potable.

Delroy rolled out from beneath the Kenworth. His white T-shirt was smeared with grease and sweat. "You OK?" he hollered to her. Beth coughed and waved her hand at him. It was only 8:30, but Delroy looked as if he'd been at it for hours. Since Beth's arrival the previous afternoon, the number of transmission parts on the floor had been reduced by half. "Your part'll be here 'bout one," Delroy told her.

"*One*," Beth repeated, anguished, but Delroy had disappeared under the engine again.

Outside, the sun had burned the dew off the Johnson grass on the high plains. Grasshoppers rattled in the borrow ditch and Beth wobbled over to a make-shift waiting area off the bay, feeling the hope of being in Santa Fe. A wiry man was seated in one of two metal folding chairs wedged between stacks of truck tires, drinking coffee out of a Styrofoam cup the same size as hers. As Beth approached, he looked out at her from over his Ray-Bans, and the travelers sized each other up. He took in her prim, tailored denim skirt and crisp linen blouse, and she his starched Levi's and plaid cotton shirt buttoned right up to his neck. His straight black hair was pulled into a ponytail from a receding hairline, but he was clean shaven, and his smile was nice enough. He had good teeth.

"I'm Beth," she said, extending her hand. His handshake was firm, respectful. She noticed the edges of a tattoo beneath the cuff of his neatly pressed shirt.

"Jimmy" he said, his voice nasal. "Jimmy Montaño. Most people call me Tito."

"That's my car over there. Water pump."

"That's my trailer outside. I'm due in Clovis tomorrow."

"I'm due in Santa Fe, soon as Delroy gets the part."

For the next hour they exchanged small talk, the stilted revelations of the marooned – he was a medium-hauler based in Lubbock; she was a nurse at an AIDS clinic in Austin. "Driving from Austin to Santa Fe, you got yourself off the main road."

"My daddy farmed cotton near Levelland. I was remembering a short cut around Lubbock."

"Short cuts are never as short as we think they are." Jimmy laughed, and when he shot his cuffs, Beth got a better look at the tattoo – a woman's bare feet on an upturned sliver of moon.

"*Tres Mujeres*," she whispered.

Delroy rolled under the truck with the last of the transmission parts.

"How'd you know?" Jimmy asked, offering more of his forearm for her inspection – the Lady of Guadalupe, a white dove on her alabaster shoulder, her face angelic, saintly, unlike the tortured woman on Adolfo's back.

Beth shrugged and willed herself to move her eyes from the Virgin tattoo. "Actually, that's where I'm headed," she told him.

Delroy fired up the truck engine. It sputtered once, then twice, filling the service bay with diesel fumes, making her head feel light, her stomach feel queasy. "Adolfo," she said. "Do you know someone named Adolfo?"

Jimmy put a steady hand on Beth's wrist as she rocked in the rusted chair. "How do you know Adolfo?" he asked.

Beth wanted to see his eyes, but they remained hidden behind the Ray-Bans. Still, she told Jimmy her story.

Jimmy nodded. "If he's going back up there to die, I know a couple of boys that'll oblige him," he said and saw terror fill Beth's eyes.

"How'd you mean?" Beth dropped her Styrofoam cup and what remained of the coffee. This was worse than AIDS. She needed Raylon. She pulled her cell phone from her pocket and checked again for service. None. Desperate, she hurled the phone against the side of the building.

"It wouldn't do you no good in the mountains anyway," Jimmy said.

Beth stomped on the remaining phone parts then kicked them toward the nearby trash bin.

Delroy backed the Kenworth out of the service bay and raced the engine. The shift out of reverse was soft like butter. The truck lurched forward. Delroy parked it next to the trailer and turned off the engine.

Beth slumped in her chair. In her mind, she saw Maggie sitting on a curb, abandoned and heartbroken, waiting for someone to find her. She gasped at the thought that this would be the best-case scenario.

Delroy brought over Jimmy's keys. "Good as new," he said to Jimmy and, to Beth, "I'll get started on yours as soon as the part gets here—"

"Change of plans, Delroy," Jimmy replied. "You get her car fixed as soon as you can, but she won't be needing it for at least a few more days. I'm taking this lady to Santa Fe."

Beth sighed abruptly in wonder, and began to sob with gratitude.

# Tilly

"I guess you saw your *pinche* friend? Tattoo Man?" The leather of Joachim's oversized utility belt squeaked as he wandered down the junk food aisle, picking up chocolate Easter eggs wrapped in colorful foil, tossing them to his brother as if they were road stones.

Aurelio caught them deftly, dropped a dozen of them onto the counter and asked Tilly, "How much."

Tilly frowned. The Vigils rarely paid for what they took. Even as children they were always in her store, expecting a handout. They had been five and six when their mother was gunned down by a drug dealer trying to steal her car. The boys went to live with an aunt who already had five children of her own to look after. In reality, the Vigils had been on the street ever since their mother's death. Tilly had a soft spot for the orphans, but now they expected her indulgence.

Joachim peeled open a Hershey bar and took a huge bite off a corner of it. "We've seen Tattoo," he offered. "He's such a lightweight these days, I could throw his skinny body all the way to Texas."

Aurelio laid a five-dollar bill on the counter trapped between his forefinger and the glass. "But we want to know if you've seen him."

Tilly was obliged to answer. "My understanding is that he was too sick to remember much about his former life."

Aurelio laughed and let go of the bill. Tilly snatched it away to the cash register. "You hear what Tilly's telling us, brother?"

Joachim nodded. "We will have to make him remember, don't you think?"

Tilly threw Aurelio's change across the counter. "Don't hurt her," she said. "The girl, I mean. If you hurt her, you'll have trouble from me."

Aurelio picked up the change carefully, coin by coin. "Don't worry," he said with quiet certainty. "We're after the man, not the girl."

## Maggie

She based her calculations on the spotty information Jeanine could provide – mode of travel and approximate time of departure; her knowledge of her mother's habits, such as typical speed and compliance with other highway laws – to calculate her mother's arrival in Tres Mujeres. If she had known about the faulty water pump or how her mother planned to narrow down the search to a particular house that sheltered her daughter in the mountain town she might have nailed it to within the very minute. As it was, she had to work within broad estimates, and figured she had at least until morning until her mother would appear and force a showdown.

She stood inside the cramped and seedy but now spotlessly clean bathroom in the trailer, holding a condom she'd dug out of her makeup bag. All she knew about sex she'd learned in a pickup truck and she hesitated now to go to what passed as a real bed, and Adolfo who waited there for her.

Her wavering had nothing to do with the safety of the act – her mother had steeped her in information about how to have safe sex in the age of AIDs and the condom she held wasn't sheepskin and it included the right sort of lubricant. It was Adolfo with his tattoo of the Virgin on his back, and her wonder that Tilly probably did not know she'd been his unwitting model.

"You drew this yourself?" Maggie had asked him earlier in the evening, tracing the inks on his back with her finger.

"You know I do all my own drawings," he'd replied.

"Yes, but you didn't ink this on yourself – not on your own back, of course…"

"I drew it, and my ink master in Honolulu transferred it to my back and did the needle work."

*And does Tilly know you have a drawing of her on your skin?*

She hadn't asked the question, only alluded to it—"You'll have to get your transfer machine back from Tilly if you're going to set up in business, right?"—but he hadn't taken the bait, possibly unaware that she was even dangling any.

Now, Adolfo lay on his back, the pretty, new Walmart sheet pulled to his chest. He lay in the halo of a thirty-watt bulb that hung from the ceiling, lighting the center of the room and throwing the edges into shadow.

"I don't know if I can do this," Adolfo whispered as she crawled onto the mattress next to him, making her intentions known with hands and mouth, both inexpert and undaunted.

"Can we just try?" she whispered back.

## Adolfo

When he entered her, he did so slowly, and with pleasure so intense he was certain with each second that passed he would never last, never please her too. Throughout his time in Austin, he'd thought he would never again hold a naked woman, never again make love, never again know this joy; it was critical to him that she felt joy as well.

And she had.

Was the release of sex, after being so long denied, anything akin to the release of pent-up memories?

Adolfo believed that it was, his memories coming now as clear and fluid and abrupt as his pleasure.

When Rachel had arrived that day, he was sitting on the trailer's bench, cleaning his equipment after finishing Rita's chop. The Vigils were sitting opposite him, arguing with two Mexican dealers over the quality of the *chiva* they were about to buy. The drugs were there on the table, amply sampled, along with the money for them, unclaimed until a disagreement was settled. All night Adolfo had felt a band around his chest growing tighter. His hair was damp with sweat, and the room had been oscillating around him, moving in and out of focus, growing blurrier as the evening progressed.

"Fever," Rachel had told him. "Come with me to my mother's house and I'll take care of you."

Adolfo had thought the idea of being nursed within Tilly's double-wide, by her daughter, was preposterous, and he'd laughed even as the argument between the Vigils and the dealers intensified and he felt the danger close around them, the heat roil inside him.

Then, suddenly, a tightly choreographed interlude: Joachim slammed his hand on the linoleum tabletop and stood, shouting, before he ran out of the trailer, as Aurelio raked money and dope into a duffle and followed him. Rachel pulled Adolfo to his feet, but before the dealers had rounded the bed, the shooting had already started. She was hit twice in the chest.

He saw her fall and he ran from that horror, out into the night, the cold air hitting his face even as the duffle hit him in the chest. Aurelio's words to him: "Hide it, Tattoo Man."

The Easter moon cast long shadows all around the clearing. Everything about him seemed to be floating.

## Maggie

"Here," Adolfo said to her, angrily stripping away the cheap, thin sheet of veneer that hid the ammo box at the

back of the closet's hiding hole. Money, drugs, and gun –
he told her everything. Everything he remembered from
that last night at the trailer. And as she perched at the
end of the shabby mattress, holding the new, clean sheet
over her naked body, she felt the horror of Adolfo's tale.
Adolfo wept at her beauty, and at the ugliness of what
was his to remember.

"You have to give this back to the Vigils," Maggie
told him.

"If I do, they could arrest me for a triple murder.
They're the law now, Maggie. It would be their word
against mine."

"Then let's get out of here before they come and *take*
these things from you." She punctuated her words by furi-
ously throwing clothes to Adolfo to put on himself, even
as she got herself dressed. Suddenly, they heard the sound
of tires on gravel. Headlights pierced the bullet holes.

Her first thought was that her mother had found
the trailer and was pulling into the clearing to reclaim
her. Then...

"Hey! Tattoo man!"

Maggie could hear the boots of a Vigil brother
crunch the gravel as they approached this sorry home
she and Adolfo had made for themselves. She reached
into the ammo box and grabbed the gun. It was cold,
and heavy – much heavier than the pistols Raylon had
taught her to shoot at the gun club. She released the clip
and counted the bullets.

"I've never fired a gun in my life," Adolfo told her.

She nodded. "I'm a pretty good shot."

He stuffed the cash and Mexican *chiva* into the duffle. "Wait here," he said.

## Adolfo

Logic. Mercy. One would influence and the other temper the Vigils' plan, whatever it was, in coming to the trailer in the dark of this late night. Surely logic and mercy would see him through this encounter with the brothers, but they quickly set on him, their blows falling like soft thuds, snow patties dropping from the limbs of spruce trees, and he knew the only reason he would survive the night was their need of him. The beating was just a warning – they needed him to tell them where their drugs and money were hidden, and this would keep him alive.

This, and Maggie, who stood on the steps of the trailer, the moon ignited behind her into eerie fluorescence. She held the gun with both hands as she descended, seeing Adolfo curled on the ground, offering no resistance to the Vigils, cursing and spitting on either side of him, poking him with their night sticks and the steel tips of their boots. Blood seeped through Adolfo's fingers into the gravel around his head. Maggie's fear was calmed by her anger. Her first shot smashed the light of the police cruiser.

For a moment, the only sound was Adolfo's rattled breathing. Lips sealed, expressionless, Maggie said nothing. Her mind worked calculations of velocity and distance. The second shot tore the epaulet on Aurelio's right shoulder. Both men dropped their sticks and backed toward the cruiser. Maggie stepped closer.

"White bitch," Joachim screamed.

"We were here to save you from him," Aurelio added.

Maggie fired once more, neatly just missing Joachim's ear. The Vigil brothers tripped backwards, slamming car doors. The cruiser ripped meadow grass and was gone.

# Maggie

The Española Hospital emergency room was empty. As she signed Adolfo in, Maggie realized how little she knew about him – neither his age, nor his birthday. All she knew about his medical history was that he had HIV. Even giving a current address was difficult. Tito's trailer, east of the highway. In the end, she put down her own address in Austin. When they asked about insurance, Maggie was left with only a blubbered answer, and tears. "I don't know if he has insurance. He was a patient of an AIDS clinic in Austin, I know that, but I don't know what they required about insurance, if they ever required it. Or if he would have had the money to buy it if they did, but I know they treated him there—"

The nurse in charge, a tall, raw-boned woman with cropped black hair, took Maggie's arm with a surprisingly gentle hand and led her into a small room behind the nurse's station. "How did this happen?" Her voice was calm and kind, but firm.

"Two men came to our trailer," Maggie said, still crying. Her hands worried the tail of her flannel shirt. Her fingernails were caked with drying blood. Adolfo's blood highlighted the lines on her palms – the heart line, the head line. The life line. "I've got to wash my hands." She could hear her mother admonishing her about safe sex. "He's got AIDS," she confessed. She'd left the diagnosis off the sign-in form.

The nurse ushered Maggie to the sink in the corner of the room, showed her how to work the water pressure with her knee, handed her a disposable scrub pack complete with brush, fingernail scraper, and cleanser. As the nurse left the room to update Adolfo's chart, Maggie began to lather her hands, working the yellow brush over her knuckles, between her fingers, and over her nail beds. She was shocked by the amount of blood that dripped pink into the metal sink.

"Your friend is badly hurt," the nurse said when she returned. "In these circumstances, I'm required to notify the police."

"Don't," Maggie pleaded, and she looked to make certain the nurse had again closed the door to the small room, and that they were alone. "The men were the police," she whispered.

# The Vigil Brothers

They brought a sledgehammer with a five-pound head and a pick with them when they returned to the trailer, an hour before sunrise. They moved silently through the meadow, except for the swish of their boots in the dew-laden grass. Inside the trailer, they were not at all cautious about the noise they made. They started with the hiding hole, where before they had found nothing but scales and a roll of plastic baggies, ripping away the plywood unceremoniously. They threw back the new sheets and blankets Maggie had purchased for the old mattress and attacked it with pocketknives, shredding its stuffing over the braided rug. They tore the built-in bench from its anchor, ripped the cupboards and sink and the non-functional toilet from the walls, turned the refrigerator on its side and smashed the tubes that were coiled on its back, in the highly unlikely case that what they were looking for had been stashed behind them.

"Now we breathe Freon!" Joachim shouted. Aurelio only shrugged and reached under the stove with his knife, slicing the brown propane tubbing with one easy stroke. Even after he'd closed the cabinet door, the propane hissed like a den of rattlesnakes on a warm March day. In the corner of the kitchen, Joachim made a ball with the paper he found in Adolfo's portfolio, relishing that it was one of the Tattoo Man's precious designs – chops and flowers and crosses and Virgins – that he

was crunching. Aurelio was out the door when Joachim struck a match to his makeshift fuse. The two of
them were driving north toward Taos when the trailer
exploded. The sound of it woke the villagers as far away
as Trampas.

# Tuesday, Holy Week,

*April, 2004*

## Tilly

Tilly's unhappy dreams were interrupted by the world trembling around her. Her double-wide shook, the windows rattled, her Milagro cross fell from the wall, and a photo of her daughters walked across her nightstand and collapsed on its face, shattering the glass. Tilly ran, terrified, from her bedroom, into the dawn and out the front of the store. Smoke and fire filled the sky north of town, and she knew instantly what had happened. In her mind she played images of faulty propane lines and the two of them asleep and unaware.

She stumbled back inside and called the fire station in Chimayó, her mouth so dry she could barely say "Tito's trailer." She left the phone dangling in her haste to throw her woolen jacket over her flannel nightgown and shove her feet into a pair of shearling slippers, the first footwear she could locate. She struggled to her car, embers from the explosion dotting the road as she drove. Afraid of becoming trapped, she parked at the turn off and hurried up the lane to the clearing on foot. Dewy grass soaked her slippers. The tops of the blackened fir trees behind the trailer were in flames. Scattered about the clearing, pieces of the Airstream smoldered like abandoned camp fires. The trailer itself was nothing more than a burning frame supported by cinder blocks. She tried to approach the ruins, but the heat repelled her. Tire tracks rutted the gravel at every step. She found slivers of a broken headlight. The Mustang, she noticed, was gone, and that brought her a measure of calm.

She heard the sirens of the firetruck and ducked quickly down the path, to return to the *tienda*. She passed the wailing truck and two police cars on her way. A third cruiser was parked at her store when she pulled into the parking lot. She saw that one of its headlights was shattered. She had neglected to lock the door to her store in her haste to get to the trailer, and the Vigils were already inside.

"My breakfast," Joachim held up the forty by its neck. His eyes were red and wild. Blood spatter dotted his shirttail, and both brothers stank of an all-night party, stale beer and sweat. Joachim took a long swig of his fresh beer.

The epaulet on Aurelio's shirt was torn, the material around his shoulder tinged with blood.

"What did you do?" Tilly demanded.

Another cruiser sped past, followed by the Channel 4 News crew's truck. Joachim swung the now-empty forty in the air like an axe. "Tattoo Man is a bag of broken bones."

"You killed him?" Tilly gasped. Bodies often appeared in the arroyos along the Rio Grande – worn and wasted junkies. Is that what they'd done? If so, where was Maggie?

"Maybe." Aurelio laughed at the thought.

Joachim extended his hand to Aurelio for a high five. "Brother broke his ribs. At least we got that." He tossed the forty bottle out the front door, into the long grass at the edge of the parking lot.

"You call us if they show up here," Aurelio commanded, grabbing two more forties from the cooler before pushing out the door after his brother.

Tilly stood her ground until the brothers had peeled out and onto the road. Then she crossed to the long grass to retrieve the empty. Holding it by its neck reminded her of the days before the *hermanos* had cleaned the dealers out, when the whole town had looked like a garbage pit. The thought that the Vigils believed Maggie and Adolfo might show up at her *tienda* was a great comfort – it meant the brothers believed their victims were still both alive. But even this did not quell her fury. She whirled and threw the empty bottle long and hard and it exploded in the middle of the asphalt.

# Beth

Her mouth was rancid when she woke up, and a blazing morning sun was streaming through the undrawn curtains. The previous night's room service cart – a half-eaten hamburger, cold French fries, and three empty mini-bottles of Jack Daniel's – was beside her bed and served to orient her. She was in Santa Fe. Her daughter was nearby.

She called for coffee, flipped on the television, showered and dressed quickly, and it was still only eight AM. The rental car wasn't due to be delivered to her hotel until nine. She sat at the small desk and rifled through the various magazines and pamphlets in their tourist-friendly leather portfolio until she found a local map. Throughout the drive from West Texas, Tito had said little about Tres Mujeres, but from what he had, Beth had become increasingly optimistic that finding Maggie would not be hard. Tres Mujeres was a small community; people there knew and looked out for each other. Locating her daughter would be a matter of flashing Maggie's photo among a close-knit group of people and asking if they'd seen the young stranger.

Beth opened her purse and foraged for her wallet, the thick stack of photos of Maggie in the plastic sleeves, one for every year of her life. She pulled the most recent one, taken at the mid-point of Maggie's junior year. Her hair was longer now, but the eyes and the smile were unmistakable.

She was sipping a cup of now-cold coffee, peering out the hotel window, looking impatiently for the rental car to pull up in the carport outside while she dialed Raylon, who was making hospital rounds. She began with an accounting the previous day, including the destruction of her cell phone.

Raylon interrupted her story. "My flight gets to Albuquerque at eight-thirty. Can you pick me up?"

"I can't wait another day, Raylon."

She heard him laugh, and it annoyed her. Then he said, "Tonight."

"Tonight? You're coming tonight? How are you able to get away, don't you have rounds—"

"Watson returned from vacation early and agreed to cover for me."

Raylon's announcement both thrilled and unnerved her. "But what if I've already found Maggie?"

"Then we'll have a party."

Beth had to close her eyes to keep her composure. A party. In one of Santa Fe's abundant restaurants. With her rescued daughter and the man she loved. They hung up and she paged through the tourist information again, looking through the list of tempting restaurants, keeping a watchful eye on the carport beneath her window, half an ear out for the television, tuned to the local news, to catch a weather report. She caught, instead, the breaking news. An Airstream trailer owned by suspected drug kingpin, Tito Montaño, had been destroyed in a fiery explosion early that morning. A photograph of Tito flashed on screen and Beth gasped. The reporter went on to give a history of the notorious trailer, the people who had died in or near it, including an eighteen-year-old honors student who'd been shot and killed there three years ago. In today's event, arson was suspected.

Then a photo of Adolfo replaced the one of Tito. There were no confirmed casualties in today's explosion, but the reporter said witnesses confirmed a young man, previously known to the area, had been living in the trailer with his girlfriend. She asked that anyone who knew the where-abouts of a man fitting Adolfo's description contact a num-ber that scrolled below his image. Beth scrambled for a pen and paper, but her hand was too unsteady and her mind too overwrought to write out the numbers before the news-cast had moved on to a different topic and they disappeared from the screen. Beth was still cursing and trying to catch her breath when the phone rang; her rental car had arrived.

# Maggie

The last time she'd been in a hospital emergency room was with her father. The Seton ER had been a madhouse – new ambulances arriving every few minutes, sirens blaring, EMTs shouting vitals at the team of nurses and doctors meeting each new gurney, racing along beside it as it was wheeled to triage. Maggie had been on guard the whole time, worried someone would forget about her dad, who'd only slipped in their kitchen and gashed a knee. Tonight was the opposite. With straight-backed chairs and hard vinyl couches, and no one but her in any of them, the emergency room waiting area looked more like a bus station at three AM than a hospital. The nurses emerged to give her regular updates on Adolfo's status, which improved every hour. Maggie curled up on a couch, and the clerk brought her a plastic-covered pillow and a thin blanket. The stress had exhausted her, but she dozed only fitfully. She was afraid for Adolfo and herself. Rio Arriba County deputies came into the area only twice with accident victims. Each time Maggie heard sirens she hid in the ladies' room until she was sure the deputies weren't the Vigils.

At sunrise, Adolfo's doctor, a short Pakistani man in his mid-fifties with curly salt-and-pepper hair and dark circles beneath his eyes, came to the waiting room and took a seat on the hard chair opposite the sofa Maggie had staked out.

"He has a broken nose, and four cracked ribs. A lung contusion, and a laceration." He moved his index finger across his forehead, to show her its location.

"What about a concussion?" Maggie asked.

The doctor shook his head. "I fixed his nose. Sewed him." Once more the doctor moved his finger across his forehead. "He's in plenty of pain, but you can take him home. Get these filled." The doctor handed Maggie two prescriptions, one for pain, the other an antibiotic.

"Why the antibiotic?" she asked, following the doctor toward the nursing station.

"He has fever. One hundred and one," the doctor replied.

Maggie put her hand on the doctor's arm, to stop him from walking away from her. "And you're worried the fever will become pneumonia?"

"That's what the antibiotics are for," the doctor told her. A nurse, the same one who'd kept the secret of Adolfo's beating from the police, leaned over the nurse's station and handed Maggie a packet of instructions along with a paper bag filled with tape and bandages. "The stitches need to come out Monday," she said, fishing a dozen single-use packets of Neosporin from a cupboard. "For the laceration," she said and dumped them into the bag, along with a box of surgical gloves. "For your protection when you clean his wounds."

Maggie nodded. She was far beyond the person she'd been just twelve hours before – now she really was his caretaker.

"May I… May I use your phone?" Maggie asked.

The nurse hesitated only a moment, then picked up the receiver and handed it to Maggie. She punched a button for an outside line. "What's the number? I have to dial it for you."

Maggie had kept the scrap of paper Rita had slipped her in the diner in her wallet. She tugged it out of her back pocket now and dictated the number to the nurse.

Rita picked up on the first ring. "Hi, Rita? I don't know if you'll remember me, we met…"

"Maggie? Thank goodness you're all right!" Rita replied.

When the nurses rolled Adolfo out in a wheel chair, his wrapped head looked like he was wearing a turban, his swollen nose was packed with gauze. He held his right arm tightly against his side. Swaddled in the thin hospital blanket, he looked like a child. Maggie didn't flinch; she had seen worse with her dad.

Outside, the bright sun seemed indifferent to their situation. Maggie drove the car around the parking lot and into the ambulance bay. Adolfo moaned when the orderly loaded him into passenger seat.

"You shouldn't have stayed," Adolfo mumbled when he and Maggie were alone in the car.

"I know," Maggie said, which made him laugh and groan in pain.

"Seriously, we can't go back to the trailer now."

"I know."

"They'll kill us both."

"I know." Maggie eased the Mustang onto highway 285. The morning traffic was light. Heavy clouds hung atop *Tres Mujeres* peaks like ground fog in an Austin winter.

## Adolfo

Rita lived in a four-room, adobe house off Bishop's Lodge Road, close enough to Tesuque Creek to hear tumbling water during the spring run-off. When the

Mustang pulled into the drive, wood smoke layered the crevasses of Tesuque Canyon.

Adolfo slung an arm over the shoulder of each of the women and held his breath as they supported him into the house. With its low ceilings and small windows, the house was warm and cozy. The aged vigas were hand-hewn. A fire crackled in the small kiva fireplace in the one corner of the room. A colorful Navajo rug in reds and blues covered the brick floor.

Adolfo gasped for air as they settled him onto the tan leather sofa, Rita fetching pillows and blankets and Maggie plumping them behind his head and tucking him in. He coughed and wiped sweat off his forehead with the back of his hand. When his lung refused to expand, a sharp pain sliced from his ribs to his shoulder. He was nauseated, and his thinking muddled, from the narcotics. Still, he was grateful for being hidden away, out of sight in a house that didn't vibrate in the wind. Their situation was clear to him. The Vigils had killed Rachel and the drug dealers in the act of stealing their dope and their money. Felony murder, they called it and, if this were Texas, they'd get a needle in their arms. He was the one who knew where the drugs and the money had ended up; he was the one who could put them away. He had to get Maggie out of this mess, and himself too, if he could. Now that the women had him tucked in, however, he dozed easily, drifting away on a narcotic cloud, into a world in which the nightmare he'd made of his life was over.

# Rita

"Honey, you've been up all night. Worried. Nervous." Rita slung an arm around Maggie's shoulders and took led her to the bathroom, which was small with a single window deeply set in the adobe. The blue and white tiles on the floor were cheerful, and the deep, footed tub made her feel relaxed just looking at it. "Let's draw you a bath."

"Yes," Maggie said, and ran to the car to retrieve their duffle bags. Clean hair, fresh clothes – it sounded like heaven. Rita filled the tub with hot water and lemon verbena oil, and Maggie sank into it gratefully, her earbuds humming Thelonious Monk.

Rita went to the kitchen to make an ice pack for Adolfo, and then took it to him where he continued to doze on the sofa. "No one knows you're here, not even my mom."

Adolfo let her place the ice on his lip and nodded. He knew how information worked on the mountain. What came to Tilly went quickly to the Vigils. The cold of the ice pack made him shiver.

Rita covered him with another Indian blanket from the side chair. "I was rude to you in the restaurant. You were a surprise." She adjusted the blanket over his feet. "Mom always thought Rachel came to the trailer to save me."

"She didn't know that Rachel and I were…" Adolfo held up his left hand, index and middle fingers together. "A pair."

Rita nodded, lips closed.

"Either way, she died because of me." Adolfo pulled the blanket to his chin. "Maybe that's why I'm here," he said in a whisper. "To set things right."

Rita pulled a chair close to the couch and sat. "There's nothing to set right. You are a victim just like Rachel. Remember, I was there." Rita pointed to the tattoo on her upper arm.

"I remember doing your tattoo. Then Rachel arrived. I don't remember much after that."

"I was outside in my car trying to get high," Rita said. "I had promised myself to stay clean for Easter, but with the dealers there, and so much smack, I couldn't stop myself. A little pop, nothing big."

Adolfo looked her in the eye. "So you saw it all?"

Rita nodded. "Joachim came out of the trailer and circled behind. Then Aurelio, with a big duffle. Then the shooting started." Rita covered her face with her hands. "Then you came out– I was so scared, and Rachel didn't come out– I ran in to get her but she—"

"She was already dead," he whispered.

Rita sobbed, nodding, her words muffled in her hands. "I just drove away."

They sat quietly in their grief.

"I have it."

Rita looked up and wiped her nose with the back of her hand.

"I have the evidence," he said. "The gun, the money. The dope. That's why they want me dead."

# Maggie

Pojoaque Drugs was located in a small shopping center. The traffic had thinned. People were putting up signs on the highway shoulder, directing the Good Friday walkers from Santa Fe to Chimayó. The red car was not great camouflage, but Adolfo needed his prescriptions and Maggie would not be deterred.

The pharmacy was a converted double-wide, narrowed more by shelving on the side-walls filled with traditional as well as herbal remedies, and it smelled of rubbing alcohol and Clorox. A small bell jingled when she opened the door and the pharmacist peered at her from behind the counter. His gray, mutton chop sideburns and the thick ponytail swaying down his back made her smile in spite of her circumstances.

"Be with you," he said and, a few moments later, he greeted her at the register. The name on his white jacket read, Freddy Rincon.

"I need these prescriptions filled." Maggie handed him the paperwork. He checked when he saw the name the doctor had scrawled. "Your address, Missy?"

She gave him her mother's address in Austin. "We're passing through," she said by way of explanation. He didn't look convinced, but he set about filling the doctor's orders. Maggie scanned the shelves for more bandages while he worked-4x4's, Kerlix, paper tape. More Neosporin. She piled her supplies on the counter then turned to the small television clearly set up for the pharmacist's convenience behind the register. She hadn't seen any TV in almost a week. Just the sound of the morning talk show host's voice made her feel normal, as if there was a day coming when this nightmare would be over.

Then a special news report interrupted the talk show. The woman reporter was standing in the clearing, the charred remains of Tito's trailer behind her. A rush of fear blotted out the reporter's words until Adolfo's picture appeared on the screen. "If you have seen this man, contact the number you see on the screen," the reporter instructed.

Maggie gripped the counter, afraid for her footing. People were looking for them. The *police* were looking for them.

The pharmacist brought two amber pill bottles to the register. "Will your insurance cover this?"

"I'm paying cash." Maggie pulled the wad of bills from her back pocket.

"A hundred and twenty dollars even," Freddy Rincon said and, when he reached for the bills, his sleeve rode up his arm, revealing a tattoo – a pale blue robe and bare feet on a golden moon – on his inner forearm.

Maggie looked again at the name tag. "You're one of them," she said. "The men who pray to God and afterward do drugs."

Freddy's eyes narrowed. "I am a man, and I pray to God," he replied. His eyes moved suddenly, from

Maggie to the glass door and the parking lot beyond. "Come quickly," he said, keeping his eyes fixed to the outside.

Maggie followed his gaze to the Rio Arriba County cruiser in the parking lot and the two officers circling her car.

Freddie raked her supplies and prescriptions into a paper bag, opened the half-door to the employee side of the pharmacy and ushered her to the back. "When you hear the bell, slip out this door. I'll occupy them long enough for you to drive away." His voice was even, as if he were accustomed to dealing with bad people.

"Yes," she agreed, holding her breath as she took the bag from Freddy. Running to her car felt like a dream, one in which she was being chased and her legs no longer worked. She held her forearm in front of her eyes as protection from the dust and tiny bits of gravel set loose by the gusts of wind. Her hands shook and she had trouble getting the key into the ignition. She slipped the car into reverse, backed up enough to get clearance around the cruiser, then eased forward in a semi-circle and was back on the highway, heading south toward Santa Fe.

The snow clouds that had blanketed Tres Mujeres started to splatter big wet flakes on Maggie's windshield. The pavement glistened. In her rearview mirror she saw the Vigils running out of the pharmacy.

# Tilly

The Vigils stormed into Tilly's store. "Get me another forty," Joachim hollered, staggering over the threshold and throwing open the door to the cooler. He reached inside and grabbed a bottle. His cheeks were flushed, the whites of his eyes blood red.

Aurelio followed – jaw knotted. Tilly knew he'd reached his limit with his brother. The collar of his uniform was stretched open by his bull neck.

"Where are they?" Tilly asked. "Adolfo and the girl?"

Aurelio glared at her, uncertain if he wanted to answer. "He wasn't hurt as bad as we thought," he said at last. "Broken nose, a few ribs. By the time we got to the hospital they were gone." He stopped short of telling her about the latest sighting at the pharmacy.

"What about the girl?" Tilly insisted. With one brother drunk and the other angry, she feared the Vigils would break their promise about Maggie.

Aurelio laughed. "The nurse in charge called her a rock. Asked the right questions, never broke down. Everything they told her, she already knew. Who would've thought it?" Aurelio leaned against the door jamb, one eye on Joachim, the other on the highway.

"No ordinary girl." Tilly smiled.

"We almost caught up with her, but she got away," Joachim added, causing his brother to clench his jaw even tighter.

Tilly backed away from his sour beer-breath. "Got away?"

Joachim belched and took a swig from his bottle, swaying into the counter.

Tilly took another step back, clearing the air around her with a wave of her hand. Adolfo hadn't been around for three years. Why were they so interested in him now?

Aurelio grabbed his brother's arm and stood him straight. "Call me when Tattoo Man shows up," he said. The ropes in his neck had vanished. His face was emotionless, as if he was threatening a pushy Peñasco dealer. He kept one hand on Joachim's arm and, with his other, pulled his brother's wrist behind his back, manhandling him toward the door like a convict being escorted to solitary.

"*Peligro*," Tilly whispered to herself. Danger... thieves... murderers.

Holding the screen open for them was a pretty woman with curly black hair and wide set eyes. She wore a blue trench coat, and matching espadrilles.

"Pardon us," Aurelio said. He pushed his brother past her and into the parking lot. Joachim stumbled to the cruiser and slumped into the passenger seat. Aurelio took a turn around the rental car, noted the Avis sticker in the rear window, and the Florida license. When he climbed into the cruiser he jotted the plate number in his notebook before he started the engine.

# Beth

Tilly recognized the woman right off. "Don't mind those boys. They've just come off duty." She invited Maggie's mother to come inside.

Beth entered the store slowly, taking in the wares as if looking for a clue. She stopped in front of Maggie's favorite breakfast cereal and moved her hand to her mouth.

"You're not from around here?" Tilly had secured herself behind the counter.

Beth shook her head, saying quietly, "No." But then she moved quickly toward the counter and stuck out her hand. "I'm Beth."

Tilly took the offer reluctantly. "Tilly."

"I'm looking for my daughter, Maggie."

Tilly felt her face flush. Pulling away from Beth's hand, she folded her arms across her chest and stepped back from the register.

"I've met a fellow named Tito. He told me that you would tell me anything I needed to know about Tres Mujeres."

"Which Tito?"

"Tito Montaño, the owner of the trailer that blew up." Beth's voice cracked, and her hands trembled.

Tilly winced as Beth said out loud the name of the drug dealer in whose home her child had died, but she recognized a mother's fear. She'd lived through everything this mother was feeling, and so much more. "They weren't near the trailer when it went up," Tilly said. "That much I can say." Tilly felt Beth's relief like a physical force. "But I haven't seen her for days."

Beth slumped against the counter.

Outside, clouds covered the sun, the first in a series of spring storms that were predicted to last through the week.

"I'm so hot," Beth gasped, shedding her trench coat. The starched collar of her white cotton blouse was wrinkled with nervous sweat. She had the same thin bones and narrow shoulders as her daughter, but Tilly assumed that, like Maggie, Beth's strength was deceptive, hidden beneath a seemingly frail frame.

"Where is she?" Beth seemed to have recollected herself.

"I don't know," Tilly said. "Truly. Word has it that Maggie drove away from the local hospital early this morning." Beth covered her mouth with her hand and Tilly added quickly, "It was Adolfo who was hurt. Beaten by the same men that blew up the trailer, I believe."

Beth's eyes widened, and color drained from her face.

Tilly's empathy was deep, but she was still conflicted. Giving up fellow *norteños*, like the Vigils, was unheard of. Also, a part of her wanted Adolfo beaten, gone. Dead. Even if, as it had turned out, her hatred of him all these years had been misdirected.

Even if, however, she wanted to tell Maggie's mother everything she knew – mother-to-mother – she had nothing of consequence to say.

# Jimmy

Being a rogue agent was not within Jimmy "Tito" Montaño's nature. He was perfectly willing to bend the rules, when the situation required it, but disobeying a direct order was beyond what his integrity would allow. This didn't mean he was above lobbying for what he wanted, or being pissed off when he didn't get it. He'd had enough of wandering West Texas backroads searching for drug dealers, when there was a direct link to a live one pinned down in New Mexico – and living in his old trailer! So he had driven the four hours from Santa Fe back to Clovis, his cell phone plugged into his ear, hotly contesting Fred Mullins's directive that he stay away from Tres Mujeres. He had dropped his load and finished reattaching the semi-trailer, and was just climbing back into the cab when his cell phone rang. El Paso.

"Well, you got your catalyst," Fred said without introduction. "Leave the truck at the dispatch center in Lubbock. There's an evening Southwest flight from Austin to Albuquerque that makes a stop in Lubbock. Don't miss it – flights that will get you where you need to go aren't a dime a dozen."

"I'm on my way. I knew the tattoo guy would make his way back there – felt it in my bones. And when I met his new girl's mother in my travels and found out he was living in my old Airstream—"

"Not anymore. The trailer's gone," Fred said. "Nobody was in it when it blew, and good thing because it's scrap metal at this point."

"Thank God. It's killed enough people. And we've little to show for it." Images of the young girl who'd been shot twice in the chest, alongside two drug dealers, played in his mind. He'd never considered Adolfo a suspect, or even a person of interest, but he was the key to resolving this case. Tito knew it in his bones. Adolfo's return, and the explosion of the trailer, confirmed what he'd long believed.

Tito drove directly to the dispatch center in Lubbock then took a cab to a hotel near Lubbock Airport, where he showered and changed his clothes before rushing to catch the plane to Albuquerque. All the aisle seats were taken so he chose a middle one, next to a tall man with a square jaw and what even Jimmy would identify as remarkably blue eyes. Once the plane was off the ground, Tito introduced himself. "James Montaño," he said.

"Raylon," the man beside him answered, offering him a firm handshake.

## Maggie

The Mustang skidded to a halt, the front wheels tearing through the grass in Rita's front lawn. Maggie ran into the house and slammed the door. She tossed the pharmacy bag across the room and onto the sofa, and braced the door with her back, holding it closed with her body. The room smelled of onions and red chiles, fried bacon, but Maggie didn't notice. Her mouth was dry and her heart pounded like a race horse.

"What's wrong?" Rita rushed quickly to her side, still holding the wooden spoon she'd been using to stir the pot of *posole* she was making.

"They blew up the trailer. I saw it on the television. Those two policemen who attacked us came back and blew it up. I know it was those two creeps." She covered her face with her hands and began to cry. Rita tried to embrace her, but Maggie pulled away. "Did you know? When I called from the hospital, did you know about the explosion?"

Rita nodded. "My mother called a few minutes before you did."

Maggie took a deep breath in an attempt to calm herself. "Those two policemen found me. At the drug store. What if they followed me?" In spite of her best efforts, Maggie's breath was coming faster than her words. "And my car! That damned red car, they'll spot it in a second—"

Rita cracked open the door and scoped out the street beyond. "Gimme your keys."

She handed them over and Rita slipped through the door. Maggie stood by the door and watched Rita's movements through the small, deep-set window.

Rita moved quickly and nearly silently to the car. She drove the Mustang alongside the house then out of sight, up the hill and, when she returned, she was picking cobwebs out of her hair.

"Your car's in the shed behind the house."

"They can't see it?" The image of the awful look on Aurelio's face when her bullet had ripped his uniform kept playing in Maggie's mind. "If they find us here, they'll blow up your house, too."

"They won't. No one knows where I live, and the car is only visible from the hill above. These guys are not mountain goats."

Maggie sighed and pointed to Rita's shoulder. "Dead spider."

Rita flicked it to the floor.

Maggie checked on Adolfo, who was now asleep in Rita's extra bedroom. The Kerlix had loosened about his head. He was breathing through his mouth and the air about him smelled metallic. Still, he was sleeping peacefully, and that was a comfort.

Rita came to the bedroom door and motioned Maggie into the kitchen. "Another couple of hours," Rita said, stirring the pot of *posole* with the long wooden spoon. "This'll cure what ails you… even fear of the Vigils."

Maggie shook her head and sat down at the table. "I am so afraid."

Rita took the seat across from Maggie and reached for her hand, but Maggie pulled away. "I shouldn't have called you. I got you involved. You, and your house… They could kill us all." She stood up and paced from the kitchen to the living room and back again. "Look, I think the best thing to do is to leave. Today, now. I can drive, we can go south, or to Austin… do it now before Adolfo can disagree. I know he wants to be here on Good Friday, but he's too sick to say no."

Rita wrapped her arms around her and led her to the couch. "Take a deep breath and be still. For the moment we are safe. The house is rented, not in my name. I have only a cell phone, and all my mail goes to a post office box. Yes, the crooked police could find me, but not today."

Maggie wanted to believe her.

"Next week or next month, we are not safe. Not as long as those guys are looking. And they won't stop looking, and here is why—"

Maggie turned her face to her new friend and waited for the explanation.

"—I'm part of this from the beginning. I was there that night. I saw Joachim run out of the trailer, then Aurelio with a big blue duffle. I saw him toss that duffle to Adolfo. I heard him tell Adolfo to hide it. I don't know, adrenaline must have kept the *chiva* out of my brain. And then, grief. When I saw that Rachel was dead, that she was killed while I was in my car skin-popping dope? Grief kept me sober after that."

Maggie touched Rita's arm. "We have it." She pointed to the bedroom. "Money, dope, a gun. We have it." And, suddenly, the whole of the nightmare became clear to her. "They're cleaning up," she said. "Getting their property back and getting rid of anyone they think kept them from it, or tried to cheat them out of it."

"And they want *me* as much as they want Adolfo," Rita said. "And the stash."

"We can turn it in. Call the police."

"Rio Arriba County? They're all crooked." Rita sighed, shaking her head. "And the Vigils are in the middle."

"Surely there's someone?" Maggie insisted.

## Beth

Raylon stepped through the rotating glass doors into the non-secure airport space and Beth ran to him. They held each other so tightly, for so long, that she failed to notice the short, neatly dressed man – dark-blue business suit, plain yellow tie, long pony tail – who was standing beside him. The short man cleared his throat to interrupt their embrace.

"I didn't think I'd see you again so soon," he said.

Beth looked at Raylon then back to Tito. "You two know each other?"

Raylon laughed. "We sat together on the plane. I told him why I was flying to Albuquerque and he said he'd heard it all before."

"I gather you didn't find your daughter?" Tito asked.

"You're dressed up," she said.

"I'm not always a truck driver."

"The reporter on the television called you a drug kingpin."

Tito smiled and handed her his card. "Don't believe everything you hear."

Beth read the card aloud. "James R. Montaño, Federal Bureau of Investigation." Beth grabbed Raylon's arm and let out a short, nervous laugh.

"My number's there"—Tito pointed to the card— "and we do need to talk." He glanced over his shoulder toward the escalator. Beth noticed two men, dressed as formally as Tito, standing off to the side, near the baggage area. "Right now, I've got people waiting."

"But…" Beth sputtered, and stepped toward him to demand an explanation.

Already a good ten feet away, Tito turned to her. "Remember, I know where you're staying."

Beth turned to Raylon, hands thrown in the air, releasing an exasperated groan loud enough to make sure Jimmy Montaño heard her. "He played me!"

"I'm sure he has a plan," Raylon soothed. "FBI agents always do. He told me the history of the trailer."

"You mean he knows where to find Maggie?"

Raylon forced a smile, hoping it might help to take the edge off. "Better yet, he knows where to find the men who are after her."

# Wednesday, Holy Week,

*April, 2004*

## Jimmy

Tito woke before his alarm went off. He'd slept restlessly, eager to move on solving a case that had plagued his dreams for three years. Looking forward to the challenge of taking on a new identity, morphing into character. He chose his clothing thoughtfully – dark suit, ostrich leather boots, bolo tie over a black silk shirt buttoned at the collar. He was going for the flashy, expensive look of someone from the mountains who'd made it elsewhere, and he'd nailed it. He arrived at Dave's Diner shortly after nine. The breakfast crowd was long gone; the last customer was at the cash register. Despite the spiked hair, her white apron over black jeans tucked into second-hand boots, he recognized Rita right away. As she was clearing the large community table, Tito took the corner booth across the room.

Rita finished wiping the with a rag that looked as if it left more germs than it cleaned up, and dropped a menu in front of Tito as she passed by his table.

"Rita."

She turned at the sound of her name and blinked at Tito for a split second before she gasped. She recovered quickly from her shock, taking a step back, folding her arms over her chest, and remarking, "One more buzzard coming home, I see."

"It's not what you think," Tito replied, and reached into the breast pocket of his suit jacket. Rita realized that, even if she ran she wasn't in good enough shape to go fast enough to get away from him. She lowered her head and dropped her arms to her side, pressing her fingers into the seams of her pants to hide her trembling. Tito hated to see such fear in her, but the restaurant was empty and he had to reveal himself to someone who might know something about where the runaways might be. He flashed his badge. "I'm not one of them," he said, and added, "Never was."

Rita's eyes were wild as she stared at the badge. "FBI?" she whispered as she slid into the seat beside him. "Really? FBI?"

"The trailer was my cover."

"Jesus Christ! You reached into your pocket, I thought you were going to shoot me." She dropped her head onto the table in relief. "Fuck," she said with a nervous laugh. "Drug dealer or FBI, either way you scare people."

"Sorry." Tito returned the badge to his pocket.

"I guess you're here about the explosion?" Rita stood and reached for the coffee thermos on the adjacent table. Her face had softened as she turned over the pre-set cups on Tito's table and poured one for each of them. "You are an answer to my prayer," she said.

Tito took a sip of his hot coffee before he answered. "Why do you say that?"

"The notorious drug dealer…" She shook her head and stirred a third packet of sugar into her coffee. "They're flashing your picture all over the news."

Tito was a trained agent, so patience came naturally to him. "There's a triple murder to close," he reminded her. And then he pounced: "With Adolfo in town, I figured the Vigils would overplay it."

Rita sat back. Of course an FBI agent knew about the comings-and-goings of someone who had to have been a suspect in that murder for almost three years now. "You know, Adolfo had nothing to do with the shootings at your place," she said.

Tito nodded. "I never thought he did," he said, and with such curt sincerity she believed him. She felt such relief she could have wept. Instead she unburdened herself, telling him every detail of her story, all she remembered from that tragic night. Tito leaned across the table to hear her as she talked – they were in a public place and, though they were the only two people in the front of the house, she was still fearful of being overheard. She made her voice even softer at the end of her tale, as she whispered, "Adolfo has it all."

Tito kept his eyes glued to his coffee cup, a blink the only indication he was thrilled with this information.

"The dope, the cash, the gun," she clarified, afraid he didn't know what she was talking about.

Tito smiled behind his mug.

"And they're hiding out at my house. Adolfo and the girl."

Back in the day, when the Vigils had made a living by robbing and killing dealers, either pulling the trigger themselves or arranging things so others would do it for them, Tito had hated the brothers. Now that they wore badges, he hated them even more. And now he could already see the Vigils' faces behind federal bars.

"Why didn't you come forward before now?"

Rita tapped her index finger against the linoleum tabletop. "I could have gotten Rachel out of there before the shooting started. Instead I chose to get high," she said. Her voice choked before she could say more.

Tito offered her the starched handkerchief from his back pocket to dry her eyes.

"Maggie wanted to leave yesterday," Rita said when she'd collected herself. "Go back to where she came from – Austin, you know? Adolfo's pretty beaten up, and she thinks it's the smartest thing to do, but he's determined to do the Good Friday walk." Rita shrugged. "She says she'll stay as long as he needs to be here."

Tito was taken by Maggie's spunk. And Adolfo's. "Is it possible for you to keep them at your house until Friday?"

Rita nodded. "No one knows where I live." She grunted. "Except you, I suppose." She looked at him to see if he was going to give anything away – like maybe he didn't know where she lived – but he didn't say anything, so she figured she'd guessed right the first time. "Anyway, no one else knows. Not even my mother."

Tito took another sip of his cooling coffee. "Your mother's not part of this, then?"

Rita shrugged again. "The Vigils hang around her like the lice they are. I'm not saying a word to her about my house guests."

Tito liked it that the others were in the dark about the whereabouts of Adolfo and the girl. His plan for arresting the Vigils was already forming. If Adolfo was determined to be at the *Santuario*, the Vigils would be there too. With a slip of the tongue, he would make sure of it.

Tito scribbled his phone numbers on a napkin and shoved it to her. "Keep them hidden until Friday. I'll be in touch before then."

Once he was out the door, Rita laughed. Leave it to an FBI agent not to burden her with an incriminating official business card the Vigils might find on her if they came looking.

# Adolfo

The hot bath water had steamed over the deep-set window and the room smelled of sage and juniper. Adolfo was stretched out in the tub, only his head above the water. Soap bubbles floated on the surface like clouds. The heat of it soothed his bruised thighs and the chest wall, and the oxys smoothed out the rest of the rough edges. The East Side Clinic would've never handed out such a luxury. Still, both he and Maggie were surprised by his overnight improvement.

This improvement in spite of the Kaposi's sarcoma lesions he'd discovered blossoming on his body when he undressed. A sure indication that his disease was progressing.

Maggie had removed the packing from his nose. The procedure caused him no pain to speak of, but his breathing remained clotted by dried blood and mucous. Maggie draped a wash cloth over his face and told him to breath in the steam. "It'll help clear your sinuses."

"Maggie," he whispered, "you saved my life." His last clear memory from the Airstream was the two of them in bed. He was amazed and grateful she'd stayed by his side even in his current state, face pounded like a piece of cheap meat for a frying pan. He felt so foolish that he'd ever underestimated her.

Maggie reached her hand into the steaming bath and tapped on one of the few places on his shoulder that wasn't black and blue. "You OK under there?" She flicked a finger at the edge of the wash cloth.

He laughed at her playfulness. "Better," he said and removed the wash cloth from his face.

She looked good in Rita's flannel shirt, open at the collar and sleeves rolled to the elbow, barefoot in tight-fitting jeans. She sat on the floor beside the tub and held a mug up to him. "I made you some tea," she said. "Lemon verbena."

Adolfo nodded and reached for the mug. He sipped from it, unsuccessfully. Tea dribbled over his contused lip. "I need a straw."

"Straws are on my list." Maggie set the mug on the tile, then knelt facing him. She reached across him for Rita's bath sponge, soaked it in the water and gently patted Adolfo's face – the line of fourteen stitches across his forehead, the ten smaller ones that held his lip, the deep-purple bruise that spread outward on each side of his nose.

"You're too good for me," he said to her, and he meant it. The whole adventure had been a mistake. He wished he could start over, never undertake it knowing so little, assuming so much, dragging Maggie along with him into danger. The Vigils would keep looking for them until they were found, and he would deserve whatever they had in mind.

But Maggie would not.

# Tilly

The sun broke through the storm clouds, making the mica-studded pavement in the *tienda*'s parking lot sparkle like sequins under a flood lamp. It was almost noon. Tilly was rearranging a display of multi-colored plastic water bottles stamped with decals of Our Lady of Guadalupe. Few of the devout who came to take the Good Friday walk from Santa Fe to the church in Chimayó would have use for them – they would bring their own water in plain and sturdy containers – but the tourists would buy them. This time of year she could count on cheap, pseudo-religious trinkets making the Easter quarter profitable.

The bell on the front door rang and Tilly turned to see Beth and Raylon walk through. The two women's eyes met as soon as she entered and they held each other's gaze, a silent plea, *Have you found her? Is Maggie safe?*

Tilly was the first to shake her head. Beth lowered her eyes at the gesture. "But I've been up since daybreak, watching the road for her car," Tilly offered. She could see Beth's eyes growing moist with despair.

Tilly glanced away from her as the bell on the front door rang again, Freddy Rincon rushing in, still wearing his white pharmacy coat.

"Need my orders of water bottles now, Tilly. I've got no help at the store today, everybody's so busy getting ready for the walk this Friday I actually had to close up to make this pickup. If I want water in the bottles, I'm going to have to fill them myself."

It was a deal between them: Tilly ordered water bottles and resold a portion of the order to Freddy; he had the staff who could sell the filled water bottles to thirsty tourists along the processional path and Tilly did not, but she was happy to take a small profit from the discount she got by piggybacking Freddy's order onto her own bulk one. Tilly nodded and retreated to her storage room to get Freddy's order. She had to move around Adolfo's chair, and his transfer machine, to pick them up.

"Thank God it's only April," Freddy called from the front of the *tienda*. "If Tito's trailer had exploded next month, it would've burned the whole town to the ground."

Tilly didn't respond, but Beth and Raylon exchanged a quick look, though they continued to stand unobtrusively by the front door.

"Hey," Freddy called out again, picking up a green bottle in one hand and a purple one in the other, and eyeing the decal of the saint stamped on their sides. "These are better than last year's. The saint is a better design than three crosses on the hill."

Again Tilly made no reply. The only noise from the small storage room was boxes being moved. "Did you see your old friend, the tattoo guy, and his new lady?" Freddy was accustomed to Tilly's reluctance for small talk, and was unaware that Beth had taken a small but decisive step in his direction. "Yeah, he's back in town, if you didn't know, and apparently already in trouble. The girl came in with two prescriptions for him. Avelox and oxys, and she bought a bunch of bandages too. Then, before I could check her out, those Vigil brothers showed up."

Tilly, who'd just emerged from the storage room carrying a double stack of boxes in her arms, stopped cold. The boxes thumped to the floor. Beth let out a strangled sound, soft but clearly distressed, and marched up behind him. "Then what?" Beth asked as Raylon moved forward and put his arm around her shoulder to steady her.

Freddy looked at the eager faces around him, unsure why they were all so interested in a tidbit of local gossip. He was unsure if he should continue to talk, but Tilly nodded, curling her fingers at him in a signal to go on.

"Well, then"—Freddy cleared his throat—"those Vigil brothers. They showed up. They had seen the girl's car in the parking lot." Freddy shuffled on his feet, uncomfortable and still bewildered at the attention his news had garnered. He shrugged. "I helped her escape out the service door. She's a pretty girl."

When he stopped speaking, Beth consciously relaxed. The motor boat sensation had started at the back of her head and she did not want to risk a headache. Not today. Not now when Maggie still hadn't been returned to her. "That girl," she said to Freddy, "is my daughter."

# Maggie

Adolfo was sleeping, snoring gently in Rita's extra bedroom. Rita was at work. Maggie had done what little laundry she and Adolfo had created in Rita's small, stacked washer/dryer unit. She'd put away the dishes in Rita's dishwasher. She'd found Rita's vacuum cleaner and swept the carpets. Her mother would have laughed to see her nervously puttering around Rita's neat house like a bored housewife, but she was desperate for something productive to do to take her mind off the drugs and the money – and the gun – that rested in a duffle bag at the back of the closet in the extra room. Something absorbing to do to take her mind off the danger. Plugging herself into her headphones or flipping through the channels on Rita's TV was no distraction at all. She'd counted the beautiful blue artisan tiles that surrounded Rita's kiva fireplace and multiplied them out into infinity and it was no use—

"Hello?"

"It's Maggie."

"OOH, Lala! Girlfriend, the cavalry's out looking for you now! I overheard my mom on the phone with Adolfo's sister and, well, OOH, LaLa to the max, you'll never guess—"

"Jeanine, stop it."

Jeanine grew immediately and uncharacteristically quiet.

DAVID SNYDER

"I mean," Maggie said, "you don't know what's going on out here. I'm in real trouble. *Real trouble*, do you understand? Stop ooh-la-la-ing me like I'm off on a lark, OK?"

Jeanine cleared her throat, unsure how to respond.

"Just tell me what you were going to tell me," Maggie said.

"Yes," Jeanine said, chastened. "Raylon. He left to go meet your mother in Santa Fe. To find you." Jeanine paused. "I – I guess I can't imagine a lot worse than my mother out looking for me. I'd be in so much trouble…"

Maggie nodded silently. Then she laughed, longing for a world in which her mother's wrath was the worst she could imagine having to endure.

## Beth

On the drive back to Santa Fe, Raylon and Beth stopped at the Sanctuario. Tilly's directions were impeccable, and the church was beautiful. The adobe structure was built in 1816 and had two courtyards, each of which was entered through an ornately carved wooden gate. Surrounding the outer courtyard was a parklike gathering area, paved with cement and flagstone through which ran the *acequia*.

"It's stunning," Raylon murmured as he and Beth walked through a gate and took a seat on one of the benches that studded the park.

Beth stiffened. "Not stunning enough to risk my daughter's life over."

Raylon had been about to put his hand on her shoulder. He stopped himself mid-gesture. "I didn't say that, Beth."

"Well, what *are* you saying? That you're happy strolling around an old churchyard like a couple of tourists while my daughter is who-knows-where? And in danger?"

"You heard what Tito told us. If he can't locate them before Friday, we can be fairly certain they'll show up here then—"

"So, you're saying we just wait till Friday! Just wait and see what happens?"

Raylon took a deep breath before he answered. "Beth, think about what you're saying. That you and I have a better chance of finding them than the FBI. We need to let the FBI do its job. Tito so much as said we could assume they were holed up somewhere and safe—"

"Safe!" Beth shoved his shoulder. They were both shocked by the force of her blow. "Safe? From whom? Those horrible Vigil brothers? From each other? Is Maggie safe from *him*?" She shoved him again. Harder. "Have you lost your mind?"

## Adolfo

Late that night, Rita and Maggie asleep, Adolfo shuffled cautiously through the house. The Easter moon lit the kitchen in a silver half-light. His ribs felt as if they'd caught a runaway tattoo gun, his nose like a baseball after a home run. He was dry-mouthed from the oxys and he rummaged through Rita's cupboards for a glass for water.

This...*adventure* had been a mistake. This much he knew, though he couldn't remember why he'd even come to Tres Mujeres. To die or to live. In Austin the medicines that kept him alive made him want to die but, *here*, he'd thought he could live on air. He turned on the faucet and let cold water pour into a coffee mug he'd found. His worst sin had been to involve Maggie in his scheme. To convince her that Tres Mujeres held the answer to all their prayers. All it had held was danger and, in some part of his fevered brain, he should have known that. Had to have known, for all his big talk, that he wasn't going to come back to a hero's banner across the main drag through town and a Welcome Home party.

He gulped the first mug full of water, then refilled it and went out the kitchen door, to the stoop that led to Rita's small patch of backyard to drink in the glow of midnight. Coyotes yipped from the hill behind the house. The cold numbed his bruised face. A meteor burned a line in the northern sky. The moon and stars seemed close, so close he felt as if he could reach through them to the time before, when he was innocent and unmarked, to the time when Tres Mujeres was just an invitation, that first time he'd joined the men in their pre-dawn march up the mountainside and his life was forever changed.

He tossed the remainder of his water into the juniper bushes off the stoop and wondered, *If given a do-over, would I be so blind? Would I recognize the* chiva *and the brotherhood as two sides of the same coin, two different parts to the same empty promise?*

Tomorrow was Holy Thursday. And Friday? He could be assured the Vigils would be there for the ceremony. Not in the *Sanctuario*, with the tourists and Easter-Sunday Catholics, but the *morada*. He knew where he could find them. Now he just had to make a plan about what to do with them when he did.

# Holy Thursday,

*April, 2004*

## Tilly

**A** leg of lamb, mint jelly, a bunch of carrots – items for the Easter meal, things she didn't carry in her own store. Tilly stood in line at the grocery store check-out, thinking about what she would say to Rita when she called. *I have treated you badly. You have turned your life around, freed yourself from the* chiva, *gotten healthy. Worked an honest job. I have been chosen as Mary again for the Good Friday procession. Will you come to the procession, too? Will you come and eat your Easter meal with me?*

"These lilies yours, too?" the cashier asked.

"Yes," Tilly told her, pushing the bouquet along the moving belt. She would call Rita as soon as she got back to the *tienda* to offer her invitation. But, before she called Rita, she would go to visit her other daughter.

The cemetery was small and, since her visit the day before, more of the plots had been tended, decorated with plastic lilies for the season, though most of the others were still overtaken by the crushed beer cans and broken pint bottles, the cigarette butts and used condoms left behind by the young people who partied along the perimeter. Still, she could tell that something else had changed as soon as she passed the genuflecting white marble angel just inside the gate – the one who watched over the Menendez family, seven of them killed by smallpox in the same year. The angel, the many small white crosses planted in rows around it, Joe Anaya's obelisk – all were unmarred. Rachel's cross, however, had been ripped from the ground and cast aside, onto a pile of road trash. Tilly gasped when she saw it and rushed to the grave. The earth on top had been torn, clawed at as if a wild animal had wanted to dig up a bone. The glass vase was shattered.

Tilly stood in shock, her head swiveling, surveying other graves, all of them untouched. All but Rachel's. Crows cawed at her from the pine trees. The cold spring air burned her throat. Pain welled in her chest and forced a wail from her throat. This was the work of the Vigils, and it was a message: *Don't interfere. You lost one daughter. If you get in our way, you'll lose the other one, too.*

## Maggie

Rita was at the restaurant, pulling the morning shift. Adolfo was in the extra bedroom, sleeping peacefully under the influence of the oxys. Maggie stood at the kitchen sink in the quiet house, rinsing their breakfast dishes. The knock at the front door startled her. She ran through the living room and peered out door's privacy hole. A well-dressed man in a dark suit and ostrich boots, hair pulled in a ponytail, stood on the small front porch.

"Who is it?" Adolfo called from the bedroom.

"I don't know," Maggie called back.

Adolfo groaned as he sat up, which made the pain in his ribs worse. "Don't do anything... let me answer it," he shouted, though it hurt even to breathe.

But Maggie had already cracked the door. "Hello," she said and, in answer, the man brought a fist-sized gold badge to her nose. It took her several seconds to realize what she was staring at. "The FBI?" She didn't know whether to feel relieved or terrified.

"You must be Maggie?" Tito replied.

Maggie nodded. "And you—"

"Tito," Adolfo said, stumbling toward the door, walking his hands across the back of the sofa to support himself.

Tito? Maggie blinked at the tidy man before her. She couldn't imagine him living in the filthy Airstream. She'd always pictured Tito with matted hair and dirt-encrusted fingernails, and a bad tattoo.

"The fuck? The FBI?" Adolfo wailed as he drew near enough to decipher Tito's badge.

Tito flipped the badge closed and replaced it in his breast pocket.

"The fucking FBI? Tito, you called me all the time to offer me your trailer? What? Was I *bait*?"

Tito shrugged. "Who can you trust?"

"Jesus," Adolfo spat. He'd made it to the end of the sofa and clutched his ribs as he lowered himself gently into the cushions. "How did you know where we were?"

Tito gave him a small smile, as if this part of the riddle should be obvious. "Rita. But don't worry. No one else knows."

Adolfo sat silently for several minutes on the sofa, not looking at Tito, and nearly afraid to look at Maggie. Then, slowly, he lifted his head and said to her, "Go ahead. Show him."

"Show him?" Maggie repeated.

"Everything."

Tito followed her to the extra bedroom where she retrieved the duffle from the back of the closet. "The 9mm has a twelve-round clip," she said. "Five were gone when Adolfo found it. I used three shooting at the Vigils."

Tito looked at her, his eyebrows raised.

"I didn't hit either of them. On purpose."

Tito nodded and picked up one of the bags of heroin. "Look," he said, pointing to an almost invisible red line along the side of the plastic wrapper. "This stuff started in Mexico, crossed the border at Columbus, was stored in a Las Cruces warehouse for three months then brought up here by the two dealers who were killed the same night Rachel died." Maggie stared at him, bewildered. "This heroin is the FBI's. Part of a sting."

"So…" Maggie stammered, "You believe us? You believe this stuff isn't ours?"

"I never said it was," Tito answered. "I know exactly who it belongs to."

Adolfo's eyes narrowed as he spoke. "It belongs to the Vigil brothers."

"I said I know that."

"Well"—Maggie was almost gleeful in her relief—"go arrest them!" Surely, if the FBI could find her and Adolfo holed up at Rita's, they would have no trouble tracking down two officers of the law in a small town like Tres Mujeres—and, with the Vigils out of the way, she and Adolfo would be out of danger. Rita, too, and Tilly. In her mind the relief and gladness multiplied geometrically.

Tito lowered himself onto the mattress and shook his head. "Problem is, right now there's no connection between this stuff and the Vigils. It's your word against theirs." He shrugged to show how flimsy a good defense attorney could make Adolfo's word seem.

"Then"—Maggie looked stricken—"what are we going to do?"

"*We*," Tito said, "aren't going to do anything. Your boyfriend here is going to make contact with the Vigils tomorrow, at the church… after the procession…

and set up a time and place for them to come pick up their"—he gestured at the contents of the duffle bag—"possessions. Once he's handed them off, then we can arrest them."

"But that's dangerous. Won't we be in danger?"

"Not if I do it in a public place," Adolfo said. He watched Tito. "Right?"

"That's right," Tito confirmed.

"We could do it at the church!" Maggie clapped her hands, feeling giddy that the whole ordeal might be over in less than twelve hours. "Tomorrow at the Sanctuary before the Veneration of the Cross!"

"You"—Tito pointed at Maggie—"need to stop using the royal *we*. You've got a mother staying at the La Fonda in Santa Fe who's going to be mighty happy to see you tonight. I'll give you a ride there right now." He paused before he added, "Adolfo's going to need a car in the morning, and I'm hoping you'll be so good as to allow him to use—"

Maggie backed away from him, toward the door, Adolfo. "I'm not going anywhere with you," she told him.

But Adolfo stopped her, his arms tight around her shoulders. "If you're with me, the Vigils could hurt us both. If I go alone, you'll be safe." Maggie tried to loosen his grip on her, but he was surprisingly strong, even in his weakened state. Even with his injuries. "This is my mess, not yours, Maggie."

# Tilly

Tilly walked into the diner after the noon rush had ended. The room smelled of thyme, sage, and chiles. The few remaining customers were scattered among tables that were waiting to be bussed, lingering over final cups of coffee. She took the single place at the end of the community table.

Rita hadn't seen her mother in almost a year, not since the previous September when they'd run in to each other unexpectedly at a produce stand halfway between Tres Mujeres and Santa Fe and found themselves at the same apple bin. Tilly's head was buried in the menu, as if she were trying to be unobserved, but the plaid coat and long braid were unmistakable. Rita squatted quickly behind the half door of the waitress station. What was she doing here? Come to lay more blame? More guilt? Had she been followed here by the Vigils—or had the Vigils put her up to leading them to her daughter? Rita fanned herself with a menu.

"You OK?" asked another waitress who was leaning around her to empty a bin of dirty dishes at the dishwashing station.

"Fine. Just feeling a little hot," Rita panted.

"Go sit down out in the restaurant. It's cooler out there. I'll bring you a glass of water."

"I'm *fine*," Rita insisted and she added, more kindly, "Thank you. But I'm fine." To prove it, she stood up, took a deep breath and straightened the apron around her waist. "See? Fine." She smiled at her co-worker, ran both of her hands through her spikey hair, and made her way into the dining room.

"Mom," she said when she got to the end of the community table.

Tilly looked up, startled. She hadn't been prepared for Rita to be so willing to approach her. She stood, slowly, and the women stared at each other for several seconds.

Then, as if there were no other course of action, they fell into each other's arms.

"Mom," Rita sighed.

"Rita," Tilly wept.

# Beth

Beth watched her daughter from across the hotel room. Raylon had graciously offered to take the room down the hall, so Beth and Maggie could be together, alone, but Maggie had given no indication that she was willing to talk at all. She was sprawled across the other double bed in the room, flipping idly through the channels on the TV, pausing to watch a commercial, of all things, here and there, never content with one show or another for more than thirty seconds. The room service tray, which Beth had ordered and which was filled with several of Maggie's favorite dishes—a cheeseburger and fries, fried chicken with mashed potatoes, cheese enchiladas—sat by the side of the bed, untouched.

Beth had tried to hug her daughter when Tito brought her to the hotel, but Maggie stiffened in her embrace. Her instinct had been, then, to be stern with her, but her anger—"Do you know the hell you've put me through!"—had been met with only a glare. Affection and fury had both failed to move Maggie, so she tried another tack: reason.

"You do understand," Beth said, "that the FBI was never going to allow an innocent bystander, a *young girl*, to act as bait in a drug bust, right?"

Maggie turned her eyes from the television screen. For a moment she was silent, so when she spoke, her thoughts were gathered and her words were crisp. "You do understand that my lover is going to risk his life tomorrow morning in order to help the FBI close a case on a crime he never committed, right?"

Beth could think of no reply. Maggie's insolent blink, and the way she then turned her eyes pointedly away from Beth and back to the television screen, indicated that Maggie's purpose had been exactly to shut her mother up. The motorboat started to purr at the back of Beth's skull. She poured herself another Jameson's to warn it away. In just a few days Maggie had grown thinner, more composed, separate, as if she was no longer a part of her mother but her own person now. "If you're not going to talk to me, Maggie, I might as well go stay with Raylon," Beth snapped at her.

"That would be fine," Maggie replied.

# Good Friday,

*April, 2004*

## Tilly

I t was still two hours before sunrise when Tilly left for the wooden church in Tres Mujeres. As she passed the *Santuario* and turned north, the Easter moon hung over the great caldera to the west. Long shadows off the fir trees striped the road. The highway was eerie— no cars, no trucks, only a lone pickup with rusted-out fenders cruising the City of Gold parking lot. Posters stapled to telephone poles gave directions to the walkers from Santa Fe to Chimayó, pointing them off the highway onto the frontage roads at dangerous intersections. Tilly was surprised that no one had yet begun the trek. The hour was ordinarily much too early for the Vigils, though this morning they would certainly be at the church, and she drove slowly through the narrow streets, alert for their cruiser. Scattered kitchen lights flickered on then off, fireflies in a mason jar, people making ready for the procession.

For most *moradas,* the meeting of Jesus and Mary involved the meeting of two statues, but following the recognition of the *penitentes* by Bishop Edwin Byrne in 1947, the Tres Mujeres chapter commemorated the event with real people. For the young men, it was an honor to be selected to represent Jesus. Often times the role led to something more—chapter leaders, deacons, stalwarts of their communities. Tilly imagined Adolfo's disappointment, waking up in the Santa Fe hospital on a breathing machine in the very hour he should have been carrying his cross. She wondered if he'd ever learned that Aurelio Vigil had stepped forward at the last minute to take his place.

She pulled into the church parking lot, the first to arrive, and turned up the heater in her car. The mere thought of the Vigils cut through her like a cold wind. Her anger—the anger of all of Tres Mujeres—had been so fierce after the shootings at Tito's trailer, but she had been the one to barge into the meeting at the *morada* and demand the men live up to their responsibilities, protect the village, clear out the Mexican drug dealers. Tilly knew her neighbors whispered that she'd overstepped her bounds, but the *penitentes* had acted. When the Vigil brothers had even become deputies her hopes—the hopes of all the people—had been so high. But the Vigils had remained outlaws, only now with their badges to shield them.

The sky above Tres Mujeres peaks had brightened. Cars slowly began rolling into the small parking lot.

Women wrapped in heavy coats and ski parkas against the early morning chill shuffled into the building. Several waved to her as she turned off her car's engine and joined them inside.

They were sixteen women, all together, a somber group. They smiled at each other, and nodded, but there was none of the usual chatter and village gossip. Lucinda, the mayor's wife, draped the white wool cloak of Mary over Tilly's shoulders. It smelled of pine straw and candle wax, and it was heavier than Tilly remembered from the last time she'd worn it.

Before she could adjust the cloak around her body, the two Chavez girls joined her in her pew. Anita was twelve, and Esperanza thirteen, gangly girls both, with long black ponytails hanging beneath matching green watch caps, but also cloaked in white. Tilly envied their age, too young to understand a mother's sorrow, even if old enough to cause it.

Tilly kissed each of them on the forehead. "I'm glad you're walking with me," she whispered to them, the same words she'd spoken her own daughters the day they'd walked with her as the Veronicas.

From inside the church, the women heard the three rifle shots break the morning air, the signal that the processions were to begin—the men from the *morada*, the women from the church. Tilly, a Veronica on each side, led the women around the church through frozen ground fog that tickled her nose like tiny feathers. Tilly had forgotten how quietly a group of women could march. Awakening crows cackled from the pine trees, as occasional whispered prayers made it to the front of the line. Tilly wondered for whom the others were praying; her prayers were for Maggie's safety, for Rita's forgiveness, for Rachel's memory.

As the women circled the church for the third time, the off-key sound of the *pita* pierced the ground fog. She heard the men reciting the *alabados* as the women rounded the back corner of the church. Tilly led the group through the back door, through the tiny sacristy and into the sanctuary. Backs to the altar, the women filled the first two pews. Tilly remained in the center aisle, a Chavez girl on either side of her.

The men entered from the front, thirteen of them, led by Felix Anaya—Jesus. Tilly had known him since he was born. His brother had been in Rachel's class. Felix was a serious kid whose greatest goal was to please his father. Now his father watched as his son became the new generation of the Brotherhood. Felix had made it up the steep hill from the *morada* into the church without faltering, no scrapes on his knees or elbows. She saw the relief on his face when he entered the church, refusing to give in to the pain in his shoulder, his broken flesh, the freezing air.

Behind him were four rows of three, Freddy Rincon in the first, carrying a six-foot cross made of juniper. Upon it, newly carved from an aspen trunk, Jesus wore a crown of thorns woven from buckthorn.

Freddy was accompanied on one side by the flute player, on the other the *rezador* leading the prayers. Four men dressed in white followed, chanting the responses to the *rezador's* prayers. Behind them came the Brothers of the Blood, five of them, barefoot, bare-chested, struggling. The morning's dampness had added weight to their whips. The tips of the yucca were dark red, the sins of the village dripped down their backs.

Tilly met Jesus in the center aisle and embraced him. Her role as Mary was to comfort her son, ask his forgiveness for everyone, but the sorrow of the previous years, and all the deaths that had come from the *chiva*, fell upon her.

As the Veronicas wiped the young man's face, one and then the other, Tilly glanced at the back of the church. There the Vigils slumped in the second-to-last row, Aurelio with his head bent, eyes closed, still hung-over from the night before, and Joachim with arms crossed over his chest, scowling against the pain the early morning light caused his bloodshot eyes—and at whatever it was that Adolfo whispered to him from the pew behind.

## Beth

Beth had risen late. The relief of finding her daughter unharmed, of having her safe with her at the hotel, had exhausted her. She'd floated to consciousness several times but each time she'd yawned, stretched, and burrowed back into Raylon's arms. Only when she reached for him and he wasn't there did she rouse herself to open her eyes, orient herself to the new day, and check the time.

"My God, it's nine-thirty!" she called, though Raylon couldn't hear her over the water running, the Easter hymn he was crooning in the shower.

"Jesus Christ is not risen today," she informed him, leaning in the jamb of the bathroom door. "We usually save that one for Sunday morning."

"Yes, of course, but don't you feel like celebrating *today*?" he asked, opening the glass door to the shower, inviting her in.

"Breakfast?" Beth asked half an hour later, as she was toweling dry. "Room service?"

"Yes," Raylon agreed. "Coffee!"

Beth laughed and slipped into the tank top and sweatpants she'd worn to sleep. "I'll ask Maggie to join us."

"Please do."

"Damn."

"What?

"She's not answering the phone."

"She's a teenager, Beth. And she's had a rough few days. She's probably still sleeping. You want me to go down the hall and wake her up?"

"I'll go."

But there was no answer to Beth's knock on the door.

And no one in the room when Beth used her own key to let herself in.

"Look, let me go downstairs. She's probably having breakfast in the coffee shop or something," Raylon said when Beth returned to his room empty-handed.

The motor boat was revving its engines at the base of Beth's skull. "You know that's not true," she said to him. "You know as well as I do exactly where she's gone."

# Maggie

The throng of tourists that milled around the outer courtyard of the *Sanctuario* were not only from the immediate area but from Albuquerque and beyond. By eleven-thirty that morning the *Sanctuario* was thick with pilgrims—backpacks and ice chests, umbrellas and aluminum lawn chairs. Snowpack sparkled on the peaks to the east, but the sun was bright, the atmosphere festive though the occasion was somber. People carried banners and placards, some homemade, others professionally, all proclaiming Christ's death and resurrection. Congregations brought along carved wooden replicas, *santos*, of their patron saints. At noon, the Veneration of the Cross would begin here at the *Sanctuario*. After that Freddy Rincon would begin the second procession, leading the people in the Stations of the Cross, around the *morada* and up the rocky path to the three crosses planted on the hill at the edge of the meadow. And, as these people were making their way up the mountain to the *morada*, Adolfo would be here in this courtyard, handing off the contents of the ammo box to those feral brothers, the Vigils—Jimmy Montaño watching, in wait. For now, Maggie stood content at the periphery of the courtyard, satisfied that she knew Adolfo's plan, that he would be safe under the eyes of the FBI while carrying it out.

That soon this whole nightmare would be over.

Rita talked with Tilly near the church steps. After the dawn procession Tilly had returned to Santa Fe to ferry her daughter and Maggie here for the Good Friday veneration, once Maggie had made her escape from the hotel and her mother's watchful eye. Maggie had been invited into their conversation, but she had demurred, wandering away to give Rita and her mother privacy.

She then noticed her own mother, her arm locked through Raylon's, walking in the elm grove on the opposite side of the courtyard. A wave of pilgrims, the woman at the head of them carrying a statue of the Virgin lashed to a hand-hewn cross, passed through the courtyard gate, merging with the larger crowd that had filled the grounds. Maggie allowed herself to be swept in among their party, through the church doors and out of her mother's line of sight. She watched her mother from a nook just inside. Her mother's gaze scanned the courtyard, and Maggie knew that if she locked eyes with her, she would come apart, so she kept her face down, hidden beneath the hood of her parka, though she was still able to watch Beth raise her hand to her mouth and take off to position herself in front of the group carrying the Virgin lashed to the *madero*. Raylon was immediately on her heels, coming up short behind her as she reached out to grab at the elbow of a young pilgrim. "Maggie!"

The young girl wheeled around, alarmed, jerking her arm away from the strange woman who'd accosted her. "Get away from me."

Beth turned, confused and appalled, to Raylon.

"I'm sorry," Raylon said to the young girl, taking Beth's arm and letting her lean on him for support.

"She looked like Maggie. She did. From behind," Beth insisted. She closed her eyes and buried her face in her hands—Maggie had been so close she could imagine she smelled her skin, her hair.

"She did," Raylon agreed. "She did."

Jimmy Montaño came up behind them. His expression was pinched, stoic. A man who, Maggie thought, anyone could recognize as another FBI agent, jogged toward Jimmy from the north side of the church, breathless, a hand rubbing his burr-cut scalp. Beth followed the line of his finger, where he was directing Jimmy to look— the Tres Mujeres peaks now covered with purple clouds.

A red Mustang pulling past the curb outside the church drew Maggie's attention. It moved slowly around the church, then up the hill toward Tres Mujeres and the *morada*. Maggie was filled with horror when an Rio Arriba County cruiser pulled out from across from the church, a deputy slumped in the driver's seat. She knew immediately what Adolfo was up to. He had decided to confront the Vigils at the *morada* beyond the protection of the FBI. She willed Jimmy or the other agent to notice this traffic, too—to make some comforting move that would tell her they had noticed…

## The Vigil Brothers

The grip on her arm was firm, the voice low and guttural, the breath on her face sour from beer and chiles. "You make a scene and you're dead."

Joachim threw Maggie into the backseat of the cruiser with a force that lifted her from the ground. Her forehead struck the inside roof and pin lights flashed on the edges of her vision. She touched the pain at her hairline and small droplets of blood stained her palm. She held her other hand over her mouth, and nose; the cruiser smelled of stale beer and fresh vomit, and she focusing on inhaling the aroma of the soap she'd bathed in that morning to keep from gagging.

"The white bitch is ready for her education," Joachim laughed, tucking himself into the passenger seat.

One hand on the steering wheel, Aurelio turned to his brother. "Stupid move, Joachim. The bitch is just going to complicate our transaction—"

"The bitch needs to learn you don't shoot at an officer of the law."

Aurelio groaned, and then he shrugged and dropped the cruiser into gear and raced the engine. When he let go of the brake, the rear tires squealed and smoked.

## Adolfo

Adolfo had parked the Mustang on the side of the road and walked down the two-track lane through the pine and fir trees to the top of the clearing. He wanted to get well into the meadow, hopefully all the way to the three crosses before the Vigils fell upon him, so he jogged quickly, weighted down by the duffle bag of drugs and money. By his body laboring against exhaustion.

The wet ground was pockmarked by the hooves of the large elk herd that frequented the meadow, and he stumbled through the unevenness, though when he heard the roar of the cruiser engine, he picked up his pace. Adolfo was even with the *morada*, a good hundred yards from the crosses, when he looked over his shoulder and saw the cruiser appear on the trail. Heavy clouds had gathered above. The air smelled like ice. The wind rattled the bare limbs of the aspen grove planted on the north side of the *morada*. He entered the no man's land between the *morada* and the crosses as the Vigils cleared the trees. Mud flying, tires slipping, the cruiser churned toward him.

Adolfo stopped and waited.

The cruiser stopped just short of him in black mud and grass. The Vigil brothers exited, one from each side of the vehicle. Joachim pulled open the back door of the car, and laughed at Adolfo's face as Maggie emerged.

Adolfo dropped the duffle bag in the grass. "Why is she here?"

High-stepping through the grass, Maggie ran to him. "I'm sorry," she cried as she fell into his arms, as if being in that meadow was her crime.

## The Vigil Brothers

They separated Maggie from Adolfo by waving a gun, the .38 that Joachim had pulled from his county-issued holster. Aurelio backed Adolfo to the three upright crosses, to a fourth cross that lay on the grass. Adolfo tripped over the *viga* and fell to the ground next to a sledgehammer and a paper sack from which spilled several dozen ten-inch galvanized spikes. "What the—"

Joachim laughed as he held the gun on Adolfo with one hand, the other arm wrapped like a steel band around Maggie's waist, bracing her backside against his hip. She squirmed and kicked but found no purchase. Joachim didn't seem to strain as he held her and the gun steady. "For you," he laughed, "because you think you are a hero, so we'll let you die like the greatest hero of all!"

"Lay down on it." Aurelio gestured at the cross. "Take your shoes off and lay down on it like you're cooperating, so we don't have to hurt your little white girlfriend."

Bruises from his previous beating made him look ghostly, beaten, but Adolfo hesitated only a moment, obeying, shaking his head at Maggie's anguished, piercing cries, but it was the sound of wheels spinning on gravel—two black Suburbans—that made Aurelio look across the meadow, to the mountain trail. Stations of the Cross had already begun. Maggie's screams echoed.

"Fuck you, Joachim," Aurelio said as the sound of approaching cars grew, "you picked up the *puta* so you shut her up. Nobody cares for this piece-of-shit tattoo man."

Joachim clutched at Maggie's neck in an attempt to shut off her air supply.

"Take your drugs, your money"—Adolfo kicked at the duffle bag that lay just out of the reach of his bare foot—"take it all and let her go!"

"You're not in charge here," Aurelio shrieked, suddenly drunker, less in control than even his brother. "Put your hand out! Put your hand out and on that viga, do it or my brother will shoot your *puta* in the head!"

"No!" Maggie bellowed, and flung all of her weight away from Joachim. It caused him to stumble but not drop her as Aurelio fell to his knees, grappled in the sack of nails and took hold of the sledgehammer, and Adolfo lay himself calmly on the cross and stretched out his hand.

A wail emerged involuntarily from Adolfo's lips as blood spurted from his palm.

"*Pendejo*," Aurelio shouted, wiping Adolfo's blood from his face, as the sound of car engines drew near and Freddy Rincon's reedy voice floated on the wind, reading the first station. "By the end of today," he continued yelling, "you will be talking smack to the worms."

Adolfo nodded at Aurelio's blood-spattered face. "You're the *pendejo*," he grunted. "I've got the virus."

Aurelio narrowed his eyes.

Adolfo started to giggle. "You know, man"—he was nearly hysterical with pain, with revenge, and it made him laugh too madly—"the virus. The HIV."

Aurelio remained paralyzed, staring at his bloody hand, feeling Adolfo's blood trickle down his face and pool at his lips.

## Beth

Jimmy put one hand to his ear, spoke quickly into what appeared to be air. Almost instantly two black Suburbans rounded the turn, screeched to a halt where the two-track lane entered the meadow, spraying gravel into the trees. Doors flung open and three agents jumped out.

The motor boat that plagued the base of Beth's skull revved its engine. "Stay here and wait," Raylon said, placing his hand on her arm, acknowledging that his request would be ignored, and the two of them took off running on a game trail that ran parallel to the meadow.

Beth's headache blotted out the sound of her footfalls, twigs snapping, Raylon's calls for her to take his arm, all sound except her own breathing, which was labored and rasping. She stopped to listen to the silence in her own head as the tableau in the meadow surrounding the *morada* came into view—a county police cruiser parked akimbo, its doors standing open; one black Suburban parked at either end of it, immobilizing it; two figures lumbering in the grass, one of them holding a twisting, wailing woman in his arms; a third figure sprawled on the ground; three crosses looming on the horizon. Her fingers dug deeply into Raylon's flesh as she recognized the twisting woman, Maggie, and her legs refused to work.

"Oh, my God," she panted and collapsed beside the trail, falling against a ponderosa pine.

Raylon crouched beside her. "Stay here," he whispered. "Stay here with me. Our job right now is to be out of their way," he told her.

Beth would have wailed, wretched cries of her frustration and fear to the surrounding mountains, but she was afraid the strain would cause the headache to blossom. To tear her skull open.

## The Vigil Brothers

Joachim extended his arm and fired. The blood from the wound in Adolfo's chest pulsed bright red. "You bastard," he said, flinging Maggie to the ground and rushing to his brother, wiping the blood from Aurelio's face with the sleeve of his uniform shirt.

Aurelio shoved his brother's hands away. "Run, you fucking idiot," he said, spinning his brother and shoving him downhill, opposite from the cars, from the direction of the approaching pilgrims, grabbing the duffle bag from where it lay at Adolfo's feet, staggering under its weight.

Maggie crawled toward Adolfo. His face was pale. Each breath sucked air into and then out of the bullet hole. She knelt beside him and, using both hands, applied pressure to the wound.

Adolfo focused his gaze on hers. "Thank you," he said. His eyes were unexpectedly clear.

The solemn crowd had now rounded the *morada* and were in full view. At the announcement of the fourth station, "Jesus meets his mother," the group erupted in a mournful song. Adolfo's face relaxed. With his voice barely audible, he joined in the singing.

> *Oh, precious loving blood,*
> *Tree of the holy cross,*
> *With this cross and flowing blood*
> *Comes our sweet Jesus.*

Maggie knew the sound, the look of death. She'd been at her father's side, after all.

## Jimmy

The wind in the treetops quieted. From only fifty yards away, the mayor's voice announced the sixth station. "Veronica wipes the face of Jesus."

"You!" Aurelio shouted. "I heard you was back, pretending to be something big."

Tito nodded, holding the .357 steady. "I had to come back to finish what we started. Drop the duffle and put up your hands." Tito cocked the hammer with his thumb. "I'm counting to three."

"You took the *chiva* like the rest of us," Aurelio screamed, holding the duffle to his chest.

"Two," Tito smiled.

## Beth

Freddie Rincon's high-pitched voice wafted uphill, through the trees—"Jesus falls for the second time." Joachim ran toward it, stumbling in the elk footprints that dotted the meadow, flailing his arms to keep his balance, the gun a useless appendage as he struggled forward.

"Three!" Jimmy shouted from the other side of the meadow and fired his Magnum into the air. Aurelio dropped to his knees, still clutching the duffle in his surrender. Joachim lurched and swiveled his head, searching for a safe direction to run.

The sound of the .357 firing caused Beth to jump to her feet. "Get down!" Raylon grabbed at her sleeve to try to pull her back to the ground.

"Maggie," Beth shouted and pushed off the ponderosa pine, heading toward the meadow. In the way of mother getting to daughter was a large, drunk man in a county police uniform, running at full speed down the mountain, a gun dangling from a panicked hand. "Son of a bitch," Beth shouted, startling him as she shoved him hard, downhill, where Raylon had to leap out of the way of his landing before jumping back in with a knee to the back of his neck, holding him immobile until one of the FBI agents arrived with handcuffs. All the while the pilgrims sang.

> *By this Divine Light,*
> *O Jesus of my soul,*
> *I take in my brotherhood*
> *Our Father Jesus.*

## Maggie

The sun dropped below the trees, and a cold shadow crept across the meadow. While Raylon and Jimmy marched their prisoners out of the meadow to the back seat of one of the black Suburbans, the *hermanos* went about the all-too familiar business of dealing with the death of a member. One of the men went to the *mora-*

*da*'s storeroom for a pair of pliers. He used them to pull the nail from Adolfo's palm. Two other men, one named Efrin, silently lifted Adolfo off his cross and carried him to a long wooden table in the chapel. The women helped Beth and Maggie to their feet and down the hill into the windowless room that contained Adolfo's body. Two bare light bulbs hung between the hand-hewn *vigas* and the air was thick with the aromas of burning piñon and boiling coffee. From the kitchen, members brought large basins filled with steaming water, smelling strongly of Clorox. Cloths were draped across their arms.

For much of the past week, Maggie had felt that she and Adolfo were alone, disconnected, the two of them against a mountain world where no one cared for them. Now she felt an intense belonging. The large, squat candles on the altar cast a wavy yellow light against the plaster walls. Carved wooden figures, representations of saints she couldn't name, stood watch. Two women— both in their sixties, thin and hardened like Tilly, with gray hair pulled back into buns and knuckles swollen from decades of hard work—began removing Adolfo's clothing, respectfully, gently, as if Adolfo were their own child, sweetly asleep. Maggie stepped toward the table where Adolfo lay, and the women moved aside to give her a place to stand while she helped them. Beth, unsure of what to do, of how to respond to her daughter's grief, her quiet dignity in the face of death, backed toward the door.

Tilly intercepted her. "You need to stay and do this with your daughter," she whispered.

Rita had joined the women removing Adolfo's clothing. When they had completed the task, she turned Maggie toward a basin of fresh water on a small, separate table and began helping her scrub the blood from her hands. Beth joined them at the basin, hands outstretched. Rita gently lifted Maggie's hands and placed them in her mother's. The small red scales falling from her fingers were Adolfo's essence, a living part of him, and when they dissolved, the swirling streaks and red streams in the water looked alive. Maggie didn't resist the washing, her mother massaging the muscles of her palms, the narrow spaces between her hand bones, the joints in her fingers, the water turning pink with Adolfo' living cells.

Mother and daughter stood over Adolfo's naked body. Rita and Tilly stood with them, as did the two older women who'd helped undress him, and, together, they began to dip their cloths into bowls of steaming water to wash him. At first nobody spoke. His muscles were already beginning to stiffen and, to Maggie, his flesh felt cold and rubbery. To her, this was not his body, not the body she had loved, not the man she had loved; this was only flesh. Still, at first, she was offended by the casualness of the older women, the clinical efficiency of her mother. But in time, one of the older women began to hum an old Catholic song, *Tantum*

*Ergo*, and Maggie felt the peace and rightness of the washing ritual envelope her.

When they turned his body over, all the women stepped back, and gasped. Stories of Adolfo's legendary tattoo had circulated about the community, but few people had ever actually seen it. Even the women who had bedded him had never been given the privilege. Only Maggie and her mother. To Maggie, the colors seemed even more vibrant under the flickering candle-light. She reached out to touch them, and only *then* did her fingers feel the ridges under the colors, the folds of the Virgin's flowing blue gown that were, in fact, the scars he'd earned during his first Good Friday as a visitor to the *morada*.

The women stood back as she traced each ridge, each line, from the Virgin's feet to her face, and there her finger stopped. Maggie stood still; she felt her breathing slow. "Tilly," she whispered.

Tilly nodded, cold with shock but not unhappy. Adolfo had designed a masterpiece for his ink artist to etch into his skin, and he had used her face to represent not his heartbreak, but the heartbreak and piety of this place.

As Beth reached her arm around her daughter, Maggie leaned against her and together they prayed for Adolfo. For each other. For all the women in the room and the men outside of it. For all the men and women in the world. Perhaps even for the Vigils.

It was the first time Beth had felt free to pray since well before her husband had died. It was the first time that praying in a community felt right since well before even that.

# Author's Note

Tres Mujeres is a fictional mountain village in northern New Mexico, a region claimed in the 1500s by Spanish conquistadors in search of "Cities of Gold," who named the region *Nuevo Mexico*. But no golden cities were found. The real attraction was the land, a combination of high-desert pasture and rugged mountains not dissimilar to Catalonia, the birthplace of most of the five hundred Spanish families that settled the region after 1670. Over the ensuing centuries these Spanish bloodlines have remained relatively intact. Unlike in Mexico, there was little intermarriage with the nearby *Tewa* and *Towa* cultures or with other Europeans. Today, Spanish remains the dominant language for many households. The surnames found in these remote villages are the same as those who settled the area—Anaya, Lopez, Montano, Tenorio. This rugged area is home to two seemingly unrelated phenomena—heroin addiction and the *Penitentes*, a lay brotherhood of the Catholic church known for their charity and acts of penitence, such as self-flagellation.

At the time of the conquest of the New World, various groups in Europe, such as the Third Order of

St. Francis, practiced some form of self-abasement. Penitence was a component of the Spanish psyche. Many have attributed the Franciscans with bringing the custom to the New World. Don Juan Onate himself performed self-flagellation in public following the victory at the Acoma Pueblo during Holy Week 1598. The same custom—along with Holy Week reenactments and processions of life-sized crosses, Madonnas, and Santos carried by barefoot penitents to the shrill sound of the flute or pita—was and still is common in Seville, Spain. But such practices by organizations of lay penitents were not seen in New Mexico and Southern Colorado until the 1830s, after Mexico had won independence and the Franciscans had been expelled. More recent scholars attribute the practices to secular priests of southern Mexico, where Aztec customs of self-mutilation were incorporated into Catholic liturgy.

The first chapter of the *Fraternidad Piadosa de los Hermanos de Nuestro Padre Jesus the Nazarene* was formed in Santa Cruz, a small village north of Santa Fe near Chimayo in 1826. In the ensuing years, chapters spread north to Taos and beyond, west to Chama and Abiquiu and east over the mountains into the high plains. Being the northern-most reaches of the Spanish empire, these remote mountain villages were often without priests, a situation that worsened with Mexican independence. In their place the lay Order became the protector of the faith, attending the sick, celebrating weddings and funerals. Initially the Order met in the churches, but as the churches fell into disrepair, the Order's meeting place became small adobe buildings, usually not far from the church and usually in a hidden valley or meadow. Called a *morada*, the meeting place became both sanctuary and town hall. In the vacuum left by the formal church, the Order's influence and responsibility grew until 1851, when Bishop Lamy, a Jesuit, became the Archbishop of Santa Fe and the official clergy and orthodoxy returned. Lamy saw the *Hermanos* as a challenge to the official church and instituted efforts to suppress it. The Order went underground and continued to thrive. Finally, in 1941, Bishop Byrne recognized the order as long as it followed specific church guidelines.

Although their membership has fallen, enclaves of the *Hermanos* live on in these mountain villages. Their practices of public penance, Holy Week processions and reenactments continue along with the art of carving wooden figures called Santos, paintings of saints on wood using vegetable dyes called *retablos*, and tin frames into which are placed religious reproductions. Seen by outsiders as an embarrassment to the church, membership demands both secrecy and great piety.

The order consists of two groups. The *Los Hermanos de los Sangre de Christo* (Brothers of the Blood) perform penitential practices including self-flagellation, binding lengths of *cholla* cactus to the chest, carrying heavy crosses which abrade and bruise the shoulders, kneeling on rocks or pebbles, cutting of the skin, and mock crucifixion where a penitent is tied to the cross with ropes, elevated until he succumbs to exhaustion. The *Los Hermanos de la Luz* (Brothers of the Light) accompany the penitents, reciting and singing prayers called *alabados*, often to the piercing tune of the flute or pita. These activities are concentrated mostly during the Lenten period, culminating on Good Friday.

Following the Second World War, the worldwide heroin trade expanded. During the 1970s, following the Vietnam War, trafficking patterns changed as Asia became a less important source. More heroin came from the south as Mexican production swelled. Mexican distributers came to the region because of its remoteness as well as its proximity to major highways— Interstate 25 running north and south, Interstate 40 east and west. Finding a home for their business, these traffickers also became local dealers, and by the 1990s these villages were plagued with violence and crime as well as addiction. Rio Arriba county had the highest death rate from drug overdose in the nation. The center of the trade was the village of Chimayo, home to the Sanctuario de Guadalupe, built in 1810 on the site of a healing spring that predated the Spanish arrival. Crimes associated with addiction were commonplace. Roadways and arroyos were trashed with used needles and syringes. Dead bodies, victims of rival drug factions, appeared in car trunks and under bridges. The traditional village lived in fear. But in 1999, the community of Chimayo, led by *la mujeres* and supported by all communities of faith including the *Penitente* Brotherhood, marched through the streets, praying for Chimayo's release from this bondage of *chiva*. Four months later, in a coordinated effort involving federal, state and local officials, the drug families and Mexican dealers were arrested, and their assets and properties confiscated.

For a time, the village was free of the despots. Violence diminished as did the crimes associated with addiction, but the addiction cycle was not broken. Northern New Mexico remained a vital link in the Mexican cartel's distribution scheme. Traffickers moved their operations to villages to the west across the Rio Grande. Many users have turned to prescription drugs, and the high number of unintentional drug deaths continues. Heroin remains. I have located the fictional village of Tres Mujeres twenty miles north of Chimayo.

Cultural anthropologists explain that land-based societies suffer generational trauma with colonization. When the United States government arrived in 1848, the *nortenos* experienced loss of land and water rights, sovereignty, traditional values, and self-esteem. This wounding continues today. Northern New Mexicans are denied access to lands that were their heritage. And as consumerism and corporate culture pervade this poor and underemployed area, this loss is ongoing. Early in the novel Tilly, a lifelong resident of Tres Mujeres, tells

Maggie the newcomer, "Everyone up here feels guilty over something." Perhaps these two seemingly disparate phenomena are not unrelated at all.

For more information on the settlement of *Nuevo Mexico* and the *Hermanos* read *My Penitente Land* by Fray Angelico Chavez. For a cogent telling of the heroin trade in New Mexico and the events in Chimayo, read *Chiva* by Clellis Glendinning.

# Get the Water Street Crime Starter Library FOR FREE

Get four, full-length ebooks – **BLOODY PARADISE, FROM ICE TO ASHES, TROPICAL ICE,** and **SING FOR THE DEAD** – plus two introductory short stories by the author of **STAINED FORTUNE** and lots more exclusive content, all for free!

Building a relationship with our readers is the very best thing about publishing. We occasionally send newsletters with details on new releases, special offers and other bits of news relating to Water Street Press.

And if you sign up to the mailing list we'll send you all this free stuff:

1. A free ebook edition of the exotic thriller **BLOODY PARADISE** – "…a spicy thriller…"

2. A free ebook edition of the crime thriller **FROM ICE TO ASHES** – "designed to shoot the ice down your spine…"

3. A free ebook edition of the eco-thriller **TROPICAL ICE** – "…well-spun, tautly written…"

4. A free ebook edition of the delightfully noir-ish mystery **SING FOR THE DEAD** – Foreword Reviews' Gold Medal winner

5. A free copy of two introductory short stores from the author of **STAINED FORTUNE** – stories that will take you on a thrill ride into the life of your favorite characters from the novel

6. Advance notice about the release of the next novel in the Clint Kennedy Series, **HARD CASH.**

You can get all this and more,
for free, just by signing up at

**https://mailchi.mp/waterstreetpressbooks.com/
waterstreetcrimemailinglist**

Did you enjoy this book? You can make a big difference for our amazing Water Street Crime authors.

Reviews are the most powerful tools in our arsenal when it comes to getting attention for our books. Much as we'd like to, we don't have the financial muscle of a New York publisher. We can't take out full-page ads in the newspaper or put posters on the subway.

(Not yet, anyway.)

But we do have something much more powerful and effective than that, and it's something that those publishers would kill to get their hands on.

A committed and loyal bunch of readers.

Honest reviews of our books help bring them to the attention of other readers.

If you've enjoyed this book we would be very grateful if you could spend just five minutes on Amazon or the online vendor of your choice leaving a review (it can be as short as you like).

Thank you very much.

# About The Author

A native Texan and physician, David Snyder lives with his wife Vicki in Santa Fe, New Mexico. Through his medical oncology practice in both West Texas and now Santa Fe, he is very familiar with the treatment of AIDS. In the early days of the crisis, medical oncologists were often the primary provider of specialty care. In his current capacity, he witnesses the health consequences of the illegal drug trade daily.

He obtained an MFA in Creative Writing for Vermont College of Fine Arts. His work has appeared in *Narrative Magazine* and *Rise Forms*. When not involved with his medical oncology practice, David is likely to be fly fishing the many streams and rivers of northern New Mexico and southern Colorado or relaxing in his home on the Greek island of Kea.

# ALSO FROM WATER STREET PRESS

Ready for more thrills?

We suggest **Stained Fortune**, by Joe Calderwood, the first in his Clint Kennedy Crime Series.

Have you read all the books in the Water Street Crime collection? Check out Water Street Press at this link and see all the amazing books we have to offer:
**https://www.waterstreetpressbooks.com**

*Enjoy this excerpt from*
**STAINED FORTUNE,**
*the first book in the Clint Kennedy Series*
*by Joe Calderwood.*

# 1

I had not planned on ending up back in jail. But when the rewards are great, the risks are often greater.

I remembered how it felt the first time I'd entered jail, the edge of fear that seemed to jab at my nerve endings like the tip of a knife—a sensation I did not find completely unpleasant. Ambition had landed me here, certainly, but I couldn't discount that the nearly carnal satisfaction of an adrenaline rush didn't have something to do with how high I was willing to aim, or how far I'd go to meet my goals.

The other inmates—six in the cell of the Mexican jail I was led to—were hard-pressed to contain their desire to pounce on me as I took my seat among them on the cold, damp concrete floor. Child molesters, rapists, robbers, murderers, assorted minor scam artists— my new compatriots, their hair gelled to porcupine points at the top of their heads, dusty feet in battered flip-flops, dark and shining eyes assessing me.

The prison housed hundreds in cramped cells like this, dungeons with a toilet as the feature at the center of the room, a dank, brown liquid coagulated at its base and a metal seat for seven or more prisoners to use—no privacy and no toilet paper. Weeds sprouted from the cracks in the concrete floor, and the small, damp room smelled of body odor and spent bodily fluids. It was clear the toilet didn't get a lot of use; the inmates pissed wherever they stood.

Pedro, Luis, Gustavo, Manuel, Jose, Carlos—I was the only one with white skin among the mix of Spanish, Mayan, and Mexican prisoners. Most spoke Spanish, or Mayan, with only a spattering of English among them, but I spoke enough Spanish to make myself understood, and to understand that their conversation was about me, and irreverent.

Fortunately for me, Mexico—unlike America in these early years of the new century—was still an aspirational country. My new prison friends appreciated American men like me: they didn't resent my fresh, new, costly clothes or my expensive haircut; they enjoyed the appearance of money, and their proximity to someone who looked like he had a lot of it.

## 2

The intent to make my fortune was what had landed me in jail the first time, but make my fortune I had, in spite of the temporary obstacle of incarceration. At just thirty-four, and with a fat bank account, I'd moved to Mérida, in the Yucatan, "The White City" named for the common color of its old buildings, and for its cleanliness. I'd bought and restored an eight- bedroom colonial mansion for my home. I spent my days drinking beer by my pool, reading a book or watching an old movie on TV, and feasting on the local dishes my houseboy, Pedro, prepared for me— *Poc Chuc* and *Papadzules*. My nights were spent drinking Scotch and making the rounds of restaurants, art galleries and the symphony that made up the vibrant cultural life of the city. The Mérida population includes the largest percentile of indigenous persons in Mexico—Mayans, most of whom were still struggling to reach even the low-est rung of the ladder their Mexican neighbors sat upon— and so I took it into my head that I would help them in their rise, though perhaps in an even more practical way than I'd been helped in mine: I'd bought three additional old colonials, each smaller than my residence, though just a few streets away, and was in the process of combining them into one building and restoring it as a school for Mayan kids. It was a deeply and not surprisingly satisfying way to spend my time, and my money.

Taavi, for one, wouldn't have been surprised. Maybe he was the one who put the idea in my head in the first place—roused himself from eternal sleep and whispered it to me in my dreams. That would have been something he would have done, if at all possible, and who was to say it wasn't?

In any case, my life was paradise, and it wasn't enough.

Who's to say what's "enough"? What is plenty for one man is paltry to another. I had wads of dollars in my pocket and stacks in my safe and rows and rows of numbers on my balance sheets, but when it came to thrills, I was poverty-stricken.

About three months after my move to Mexico, in the early spring of 2008, I volunteered as a worker for the Yucatan elections—the one hundred and six "municipal presidents", or mayors as we call them in the U.S., that were to be elected that May. Those few weeks of volunteer work consisted mostly of answering phones in various campaign headquarters, posting yard signs where they were permitted—and sometimes where they were not permitted, approaching area business people with a fundraising pitch on behalf of the resident power brokers and decision makers. You could call me a "people person". From the time I was a kid, I could always pick out the ones who would be most beneficial to know. I worked my ass off for the local pols and, by the time the elections were over, I had a whole new group of friends. Politics is an inherently dirty business and the pollution among the Mexican political class is deservedly legendary; I figured someone in that crowd could get me into a little bit of much-needed trouble.

# 3

My trouble came with a name: Alvaro.

I met Alvaro—met him *formally*—at the victory party for the candidate in Mérida's Third District. He— Alvaro, not the candidate; the candidate was a forgettable little puke who would later be indicted for removing his opponent's advertising materials and exchanging cash for voting cards—was a solid six feet tall, with a body of lean muscle and a head of wavy, thick black hair. Even at first glance he seemed too lithe and graceful – too *physical* – to be a politician. Periodically he'd throw an arm around the smaller but exceptionally beautiful man at his side; the way he looked down at his companion, the smile he gave him, made me wonder if they were a couple. Both of them were surrounded by the circle of spectators who'd gathered around Alvaro, a crowd of men and women who looked up at Alvaro less as just another guest at the victory party but as if they were his fans. There were a few people among that crowd who looked too alert and wary to be simply guests; they looked like Secret Service guys if Secret Service guys routinely dressed in Irish linen guayaberas.

"Do you know who that is?"

"What?" I turned to the Mayan who'd been on the candidate's PR team. I didn't catch his name, but he looked enough like Taavi to draw me to him when I'd first arrived at the party and he'd taken it upon himself to give me the lay of the land – point out the important people I might like to know.

He gestured now toward Alvaro with the hand that held his frothy cocktail. "You think you recognize him, don't you? He's Alvaro Moreno, the bullfighter – not as well-known as his brother, Oscar, but Alvaro's the one who stabbed and killed the Intimidator."

I nodded. "I've never been to a bullfight in my life."

# 4

"Politicians and bullfighters, there is no difference between them," Alvaro told the crowd. "If you are a bullfighter, the bull is your opponent. He is the one you are trying to beat in the race, the one you do not want to lose the election to, hmmm?" he continued, and the people around him chuckled. "And everything a bullfighter does, every move he makes, is to do one of three things – distract his opponent, so the opponent is confused and can't fight back as well; anger his opponent, so the opponent makes a stupid mistake; cause injury to his opponent, so the spectators will see the bullfighter is strong and his opponent, this massive animal, is weak." By the time he finished, the people around him were laughing in earnest. He didn't need to twist to one side as if to dodge attack, his hands holding an imaginary cape, to keep his audience captive; that flourish at the end was all showmanship.

But when he'd twisted he'd ended up directly in front of me.

I stretched my hand out to him. "I'm Clint Kennedy. New to the area –"

Alvaro put up a hand and let his black eyes wander over my white skin, blonde hair, blue eyes. "New to the area? Who would have guessed such a thing?" he asked, sending the people who were still gathered around him into another gale of laughter.

I might have been put off – distracted – by his greeting, but that was just what he wanted.

"I've never been to a bullfight. I'd love to see you in the ring."

"You would?" he laughed, and he grabbed the beautiful man who'd been standing near to him and kissed him on the neck. "Then what do you say, Javier? I fight again in, what is it? Two weeks? Should we invite this Mister Clint Kennedy to be our guest?"

Javier shrugged, but he smiled as well. "I think Mister Clint Kennedy would like that, Alvaro."

"Then that's what we will do!" Alvaro boomed. He reached out at last to take the hand I had offered him. "Pleased to meet you, Clint. Call me Alvaro – and this is Javier, my brother- in-law."

*Brother-in-law*, I thought as I began to loosen my hand from Alvaro's grip in order to shake hands with Javier. *This relationship might be more complicated than I assumed...*

But I didn't get to either finish the thought or offer Javier my hand. Alvaro kept his fist tight over mine and yanked me toward him to whisper in my ear, "I know who you are, Mister Clint Kennedy."